H

HANNAH
GOES TO WAR

Phil Carradice

To Megan
With Best Wishes

Phil Carradice

PONT

First Impression—2005

ISBN 1 84323 461 0

This book is published with the financial support of the Welsh Books Council.

Printed in Wales at
Gomer Press, Llandysul, Ceredigion

To the staff and pupils of the schools who helped – with advice and ideas – in the making of this book:

Bishopston Comprehensive School
Clwyd Community Primary School, Swansea
St Joseph's R.C. Primary School, Clydach
Markham Primary School

Chapter One

'What time is it?' asked Hannah.

She was sitting on a grassy bank at the edge of the golf course, gazing out over the wide expanse of Langland Bay. There wasn't a breath of wind and the waves on the beach below made barely a sound as they ran up over the sand and rocks.

Hannah was wearing her best Sunday dress. She liked the feel of it, soft and silky against her skin, but still wished she could be wearing trousers like the boys. Her mother always called her a tomboy and Hannah supposed that she was right. She would normally have been dressed in trousers or shorts but today, being a Sunday, she'd had no option other than to wear the dress.

'Jack, did you hear me? What's the time?'

Jack Davies sighed and sat up. He pulled back his shirtsleeve and glanced at his new wristwatch. He was proud of the watch. His big brother Tommy had given it to him as an early birthday present before going off on the annual Territorial Camp.

The fortnight camp, something that had been going on for as long as anyone could remember, had already turned into a month-long period of intensive training as the crisis in Europe had deepened. Hannah sometimes wondered when Jack would next see his brother again, but she said nothing to her friend.

'It's ten o'clock,' Jack announced. 'Why?'

Hannah shrugged.

'I just want to be home by eleven. You know Mr Chamberlain is going to speak on the wireless?'

Jack nodded and glanced towards the third member of the group. Peter Longdale had said barely a word all morning. He lay on his back, chewing a piece of marram grass, eyes tightly shut and his mind far away.

'What about you, Peter?' asked Jack. 'Are you going to listen to the Prime Minister?'

'Of course he is,' Hannah interrupted. 'So should you. We all need to know what's going to happen.'

Jack snorted and jumped to his feet.

'Oh, Hannah Roberts, sometimes you are so naïve! You know exactly what's going to happen. Mr Chamberlain will wave his piece of paper in the air and shout – what was it? – "peace in our time". Old Hitler will back down. He isn't stupid, he doesn't want war.'

Nobody spoke. High above them a twin-engine aeroplane droned through the cloudless sky, heading out over the Bristol Channel. It was all so peaceful and the threat of war seemed far away – as far away as Poland where, even now, men were fighting and dying under the same summer sun.

'Nobody knows what's going to happen,' said Peter, suddenly, 'but I've got a bad feeling about it all.'

He still hadn't opened his eyes but his words seemed to cast a gloom over the whole morning. It was as if the black-shirted Nazi hordes had suddenly stormed ashore onto the beach below them.

'I'll tell you what,' Peter continued, 'if war does come, then Swansea's going to make a great target for the German bombers.'

'What do you mean?' asked Hannah.

Peter opened his eyes and rolled over onto his side. Carefully he propped himself up on his elbow and gazed at his friends over the rim of his glasses.

'Swansea,' he declared.

He gestured over his shoulder. The hill on the other side of the beach hid the town from view but they all knew it was there, sprawled around the bay a mile or so to the east. Peter grimaced.

'It's a major industrial centre, isn't it? One of the most important in Wales. Swansea's got plants that make copper, tin, lead and steel. At Llandarcey there's one of the biggest oil refineries in the whole of the British Isles. And just think of all the coal and grain that goes out from Swansea docks.'

He paused, then shrugged and lay back on the grass. Hannah and Jack glanced briefly at each other, and then turned towards their friend.

'Put like that,' said Hannah, 'I suppose it would make a great target.'

She tried to think about the stories she had read in her mother's *Daily Mail*; stories about German bombers in the recent war in Spain. They had destroyed one town, she had read. Totally wiped it out. But she couldn't quite remember the name. Guernia? Guernica? Something like that. She certainly didn't fancy the same thing happening in south Wales.

'Well,' she shrugged, 'I suppose we'll be safe enough out here in Mumbles.'

She didn't say anything about Jack's brother in the Territorials, Britain's part-time soldiers. Hannah didn't know Tommy very well but, like thousands of other young men, he had joined the 'Terriers' at the time of the Munich Crisis last year. He would be fighting soon enough if war should come.

She didn't mention Peter's father, either. He was a policeman and would be in the thick of the action if bombers ever appeared over the town. Even Mary, Peter's beautiful sister, a remote and distant figure with skin like alabaster, worked in Swansea at an office in the docks. And Peter had just said what a great target those docks would make.

Thank goodness there's just Mum and me in our house, thought Hannah. At least there were fewer people to worry about. She thought back to her dead father, a father she could barely remember. Even so, the thought of him was still too close for comfort and she quickly pushed the image away.

Suddenly, Hannah stood up. Down on the sands, close to the rocks at the far side of the bay, a girl was moving, coming in their direction. Hannah pointed.

'Look. Isn't that Helen Lewis?'

The others followed her arm. A slim, blonde girl was walking along the tide line, staring down at the seaweed and rubbish that had been thrown up by the waves.

'I shouldn't think she's seen beaches like this before,' drawled Jack. 'Or not many, anyway.'

Hannah nodded. Helen Lewis was from London and had come to Wales only a few weeks before. Hannah supposed she was the first of the evacuees they had been hearing so much about. The whole process of evacuation intrigued her. The government had decided that children – and, in some cases, mothers too – should be sent away from high-risk areas like London and Birmingham to quieter parts of the country. In that way they would avoid being bombed and killed if war should come.

One or two families had arrived the previous year, in 1938, around the time of the Munich Crisis, but they had soon slipped back to their homes once they'd realised there was not going to be a war. If war should start today, thought Hannah, there might be hundreds of evacuees like Helen coming to Mumbles.

'We ought to go and speak to her,' she said, pointing once more towards the girl on the beach. 'What do you think?'

Jack shrugged. Peter said nothing.

'I mean, she doesn't really know anybody down here, does she? She's been here for three or four weeks now but nobody seems to have made friends with her. Not that I can see.'

It was hardly surprising. The summer holidays had come and Hannah and her friends had been more interested in cycling off to the Gower Peninsula for the day or swimming here at Langland Bay than they

11

had been in making friends with a strange girl whose accent they could barely understand.

Hannah hadn't thought about it before but, suddenly, she was very conscious of how Helen must be feeling, miles away from family and friends. Peter smiled at her, almost as if he could read her mind.

'Feeling guilty, Hannah?' he said, levering himself up onto his feet.

Together, they stared across the beach. As they watched, the girl on the foreshore suddenly glanced up at them. Hannah raised her hand to wave but before she could do so the girl turned away and went back the way she had come.

'Come on,' said Jack. 'If Hannah wants to hear old Grumble Guts on the wireless we'd better get going.'

They walked towards their bicycles which were lying against the golf club fence and wheeled them along the sandy track. There was nobody on the course, Hannah noticed. It was so unusual for a Sunday morning and she supposed that all the golfers were at home, waiting to hear Mr Chamberlain's message.

They cycled past Langland Bay Hotel and along the road, away from the sea. The pull up from the beach was hard. Once they had crested the ridge, however, it was just an easy freewheel down the hill into Mumbles. The small seaside town, only a few miles to the west of Swansea, seemed a world away from the ugly urban sprawl of their industrial neighbour. But tall columns of smoke from Swansea's chimneys always seemed to hover like giant fingers above the bay.

Mumbles, that morning, was peaceful and still. On fine weekends like this the place should have been full of day trippers from Swansea and the nearby valleys. They should have come pouring off the tram that ran along the seafront from Swansea. Obviously, today they had decided to stay at home.

As the three friends swept down the hill into town they passed the occasional old man out for a morning stroll and, in the grounds of Oystermouth Castle, a group of young children. They were singing.

> 'Under the spreading chestnut tree
> Neville Chamberlain said to me
> If you want to get your gasmasks free
> Join the blinkin' ARP.'

Hannah grinned. Air Raid Precaution Wardens had been at work in Swansea for several months now, all part of the government's preparations for war. Hannah hadn't seen many of them out here in Mumbles, however. Just like she'd heard about blackout precautions and air-raid shelters – but she hadn't seen any of them yet. Gasmasks, yes; they had been issued during the Munich Crisis, but she'd only tried hers on once. It smelled of rubber and made her sick. It would be easier and better to face a gas attack, she had decided.

When she arrived home, Hannah propped her bike against the railings at the front of the house and skipped easily up the path. Her mother was in the kitchen and the wireless was already on.

'Hello, dear,' her mother called. 'You're just in time.'

Hannah smiled at her. Mrs Roberts had dark bags under her eyes and her normally bright voice was low and troubled. She had not slept well last night. Hannah sat alongside her and they held hands. Her mother's palms, Hannah noticed, were damp and sweaty.

They waited, quietly, on the settee, tension gathering like winter mist in the small room. Finally, however, Hannah heard the announcer's ominous voice across the airwaves.

'In about ten minutes, that is at 11.15, the Prime Minister will broadcast to the nation. Please stand by.'

Mrs Roberts glanced at Hannah and grimaced. She seemed to know already that the news would be bad.

*   *   *

'So that's it, then,' said Peter. 'We're at war.'

He and Hannah were standing at the landward end of the Mumbles Pier, the long iron walkway that reached out like a bridge over the waves of the Bristol Channel. Hannah and her mother often came here to watch the paddle steamers and once a year they took a trip from the pier across to Weston-Super-Mare or Ilfracombe on the English side of the Channel. There were no paddle steamers today, however, and all was quiet and still; a far cry from the death and destruction that had just been unleashed upon the world.

'What do you think will happen?' asked Hannah. 'I mean, how is it going to affect us, do you think?'

Peter shrugged.

'We'll be okay. Lots of people – people like Jack's brother Tommy – will have to go off and fight, I suppose. And I think the enemy could try and bomb Swansea. But for us? Well, we're still young, aren't we? We'll just have to stay here and carry on going to school.'

He grinned at Hannah and shrugged.

'Maybe if the war lasts for five or six years, maybe then we'll have to join up. Or at least I will. I don't suppose girls will be called on to fight.'

Hannah snorted. Blow that, she thought. If people like Peter were going to fight she'd go as well. But that was all in the future. For now, they would have to wait and see.

They paid their entrance fee and walked out along the pier. Normally it would have been crowded with fishermen and idlers but there was nobody here today. They had the place to themselves.

'Where's Jack got to?' Hannah asked as they leaned on the railings and stared into the silent sea.

'You know his father's been appointed as an ARP warden? Well, now he's got something to do at last. He's probably lecturing Jack right now on how to behave if the Germans bomb the pier this afternoon.'

Hannah laughed. It was good that they could still have fun even if, for most adults, it seemed as if the end of the world had arrived.

'So soon after the last war,' her mother had sighed

once the Prime Minister had finished his broadcast and she'd switched off the wireless. 'It was only twenty years ago my father and brother fought the war to end all wars. And now, here we are again, at war with Germany.'

It was all that horrible Hitler's fault, Hannah decided. Him and his Nazis. They had always seemed so funny up till now. She remembered sitting in the Plaza Cinema in Swansea only a few weeks ago, laughing as the Pathe Newsreel showed goose-stepping Nazi troops on some parade or other. They had looked ridiculous, marching like that. And their silly straight-arm salute? How could they possibly spell danger to the whole world? Well, now she knew.

'We should have stopped him last year,' said Peter, kicking off a piece of splintered planking and toeing it into the sea.

'What?'

'Last year. We should have stopped Hitler then, when he marched into Czechoslovakia. But what did we do? Chamberlain flew to Munich and came back claiming to have secured peace for ever.'

He shook his head and spun around, resting his elbows on the rail.

'My dad says Chamberlain is just an appeaser.'

Hannah stared at him. She liked to hear Peter talk like this but she couldn't always follow what he meant.

'Appeasement!' Peter continued. 'That's what Chamberlain and his lot are into. Keep Hitler happy at all costs. Give him Czechoslovakia, let him walk into Austria. As if they couldn't guess he'd want more.'

He'd certainly wanted more, Hannah decided. He'd wanted Poland for a start. Twelve months after Chamberlain had met Hitler at Munich had come the second crisis. Only this time, Britain and France had called his bluff. So now it was war and God only knew how it would affect them all. She thought back to the slow, sad tones of Mr Chamberlain on the wireless.

'This morning,' the Prime Minister had intoned, 'the British Ambassador handed the German Government a final note stating that unless we heard from them by eleven o'clock that they were prepared at once to withdraw their troops from Poland, a state of war would exist between us. I have to tell you now that no such undertaking has been received and that consequently this country is at war with Germany.'

Hannah knew that this moment, this day, marked a crossroads in her life, that nothing would ever feel quite the same again. A great wave of sadness swept over her and, suddenly, she had to fight to keep back the tears.

'Look,' said Peter, 'there's Jack.'

Hannah swung around, following the direction of Peter's outstretched arm. Jack Davies was sprinting along the seafront towards the pier, waving and shouting.

'What's he saying?'

Peter shook his head.

'Blowed if I know. It's too far away. And you know he mumbles like anything. Mumbles? Get it?'

Hannah frowned at her friend's bad joke and soon Jack came charging up the pier towards them. His hair was dishevelled and his eyes glinted with excitement.

'Have you heard the news?' he called.

Peter shrugged and spread his arms wide. He seemed suddenly very old and knowledgeable.

'Now which piece of news do you mean? That Hitler's invaded Poland? Or that we're at war with Germany?'

Jack came to a halt in front of them and stared hard at Peter.

'No, you ass. About school.'

This was new, Hannah thought. It was different anyway.

'What about school?'

'Only that they've closed it. All the schools in Swansea – all across Britain, I shouldn't wonder – have been closed for a week. In case there's a sudden air raid, I suppose.'

Jack danced around his two friends, jumping up and down as if he was demented.

'See, the war isn't so bad after all. I suppose they'll open all the schools again pretty soon but for now, well, it's an extra week's holiday, isn't it? Can't be half bad.'

That was true, Hannah thought. She grinned and in her head began to plan how she would enjoy her unexpected break. Her sadness had gone and she was suddenly happy again.

'Tell you what,' she said. 'Let's go to Conti's Café and get an ice cream to celebrate.'

The three friends linked arms and went off down the pier in the warm September sunshine.

Chapter Two

Jack, Peter and Hannah sat at the dining-room table, quietly sorting through Jack's cigarette card collection. Outside, it was already dark and the blackout curtains had been up at the windows for the past half hour. The gas lamp guttered and stuttered in the corner and from the kitchen came the sound of the wireless playing.

Hannah listened with half an ear to the music. It was Gracie Fields singing 'Wish Me Luck as You Wave me Goodbye' and Hannah smiled as she heard Jack's mother singing along with the chorus. The house felt comfortable and safe. *Children's Hour* had just finished – hardly surprising, Hannah thought, now that the programme had been cut back to thirty minutes. They hadn't changed the name, however. Perhaps *Children's Half Hour* just didn't sound right.

'Cup of cocoa, everyone?' asked Jack's mother, coming in from the kitchen.

'Thanks, Mum,' said Jack.

Peter smiled, took his cup off the tray and went back to the card collection. Jack had hundreds of the picture cards, everything from Aeroplanes and Footballers to Motor Cars and Film Stars. Pride of place, however, was his ARP Collection.

'Look at this one,' Jack said, holding up one particular card. 'It shows you how to adjust your gas mask.'

Peter shook his head.

'A bit ghoulish, don't you think? I know your dad's the ARP Warden, Jack, but personally I think the footballers are a lot more interesting.'

As Peter and Jack began to argue about the card collection, Hannah sat back in her chair and closed her eyes. Cigarette cards didn't really interest her, apart from the odd film star or sports card, and she needed the time to think.

The war had been going for three months now and apart from a few minor inconveniences like changes to radio programmes, very little seemed to have happened.

Despite the dire warnings of the government and people like Jack's father, who seemed to spend most of his time going around shouting things like 'Put that light out', it didn't really seem any different from peacetime. Jack's brother Tommy had gone to France with the British Expeditionary Force but as yet he, like everyone else, had seen very little action.

'A phoney war,' Hannah's mother had called it.

Phoney war it might have been but Mrs Roberts had already found herself a job in a Swansea factory. Turning pots and pans into guns and shells, she told Hannah.

'It'll mean working longer hours,' she said, 'and a journey into town on the tram each day. But at least it will give us more money.'

That was always welcome, Hannah thought. She knew how hard her mother had to work to keep the roof over their heads.

'What time is it, Jack?' Hannah asked suddenly.

She wanted to be home to prepare tea. Her mother would have been hard at it all day and Hannah knew that she would be very tired when she finally got in from work.

'Just six,' Jack announced. 'You going already?'

Hannah nodded and picked up her coat.

'Yes. I'll see you in school tomorrow.'

She slipped into the hallway, made sure there were no lights showing and went out of the front door. It was so strange, she thought. Everything was dark, dark like the grave, with no lights anywhere, not here in Mumbles and certainly not across the bay in the industrial towns of Swansea and Port Talbot. The blackout certainly seemed to be working.

She went down the hill and in two minutes arrived home. It would be Christmas soon, she thought, and wondered if the festive season would be different this year. Pulling the blackout curtains firmly shut, she turned on the gaslight and began to wonder what she should make for tea.

*   *   *

Hannah met Jack and Peter on the way to school the following day.

'You should have stayed last night,' Jack crowed. 'When my dad came home he had some oranges he'd got from the docks in Swansea. They were lovely and juicy.'

Fruit like oranges and bananas were already

22

scarce, and there were rumours that the government might even introduce food rationing once Christmas was over. It was all to do with the German U-boats that were sinking British merchant ships out in the Atlantic – or, at least, that's what Hannah had read in last week's *Daily Mail*.

She glanced at Jack's small, round face and shrugged. Sometimes, she thought, he could be so full of himself. She was upset that she had missed the oranges but knew that she had done the right thing by going home early. Her mother had been pleased to have tea made for her.

'Never mind,' said Peter, suddenly. 'I've saved you half of mine.'

He held out a neatly sliced orange, wrapped up in a piece of greaseproof paper. Hannah took it, smiled at her friend and put it in her pocket for break time.

'Look!' said Jack. 'Something's happening over there.'

They were approaching the school playground. A large crowd had gathered together just outside the gates, spilling over off the pavement onto the road.

'Listen to that,' said Peter. 'It's Godfrey Scrivens. You can't mistake that horrible weedy voice.'

Hannah grinned. Peter was right. She could hear the thin, nasal whine above the mumbling of the crowd. Tall and gawky, Godfrey Scrivens was the school bully, someone who loved nothing better than to throw his weight about, usually in the direction of people a lot weaker or younger than himself.

Craning her neck to see properly, Hannah picked

out Godfrey at the front of the crowd. He was jumping up and down in excitement, pointing his finger and shouting. His anger seemed to be directed at three girls who were huddled back against the high school wall. The crowd of onlookers stood and stared, a little uneasily, Hannah thought, at the bully and his two cronies.

' 'Vacees!' Godfrey was shouting. 'Dirty stinking 'vacees.'

If it hadn't been so horrible, Hannah knew that the scene would have been quite funny. Godfrey was dancing like a marionette across the space in front of the crowd, glaring into the eyes of each of the girls in turn. One of them was Helen Lewis, the evacuee they had seen on the beach the day that war broke out.

'Dirty 'vacees,' Godfrey screamed. 'They've got nits. They don't have baths like we do. All 'vacees smell.'

He turned to grin at the onlookers. A few forced laughs echoed along the ranks.

'They don't belong here,' the bully continued, turning again to face his victims. 'Go back to London, you dirty smelly 'vacees'. Just make sure you have a bath before you catch the train.'

He laughed, the sound loud and shrill, and raised a hand to poke his finger into Helen's shoulder. At that moment an arm seemed to shoot out from the crowd, grabbing the bully's hand and twisting it downwards.

'Ow!' squealed Godfrey, trying desperately to turn and wrench his arm free.

He was held in a grip of iron. Finding that he could

24

not escape, he stared helplessly up into the eyes of his assailant. It was Peter Longdale.

'Leave her alone!' Peter hissed.

He pulled Godfrey to one side and eased himself between the bully and Helen.

'She hasn't done anything to you. None of them have. Just leave them all alone.'

Peter's green eyes glittered behind the lenses of his glasses. His gaze was steady and direct. Godfrey Scrivens stood half a head taller than Peter but there was something in the posture of the shorter boy, something hard and unafraid. And the bully sensed it. He let his eyes drop and backed away. Peter Longdale was still holding his arm, however, and before he knew what was happening, Godfrey found himself forced up onto his toes, trying hard to keep his balance and dignity.

'We're only having a bit of fun,' he whimpered. 'We're not hurting anyone.'

'No? What about them?'

Peter gestured towards the three girls. Godfrey seized his chance and pulled his arm free. He fell back against the front rank of onlookers and then stumbled across to join his friends. Hannah slipped out of the crowd and stood alongside Helen Lewis.

'Are you all right?' she asked, quietly.

The blonde girl nodded.

'Yes thanks,' she said. 'At least, we are now – thanks to your friend.'

Hannah smiled at Helen and her companions. The other two girls were evacuees who'd arrived during the past few months. They were younger than Helen, perhaps seven or eight, and were clearly terrified by what had just been going on.

There was a sudden flurry of movement and Jack pushed himself to the front of the crowd.

'It's all over,' he called, importantly. 'Clear off, all of you.'

There were a few catcalls and comments but, slowly, the group began to break up and drift away into the playground.

'Late as usual, Jack?' said Peter, his voice low and measured.

Jack grinned and puffed out his chest.

'We showed him, eh, Peter?'

Hannah shook her head. Whatever else you might say about Jack, you could never accuse him of false modesty.

'Oh, yes,' she said. '*We* certainly did.'

Jack missed the point completely and stared after the retreating back of Godfrey Scrivens. The bully and his two friends reached the school gates, then Godfrey spun suddenly around and pointed.

'You wait, Peter Longdale. I'll get you for this.'

Peter smiled, distantly, and held the bully's gaze until the taller boy eventually broke away and sauntered off into the playground. Peter turned around to face Helen.

'What was all that about?' he asked.

Helen shrugged. Now that the crisis was over, reaction had quickly set in and she was shaking, tears obviously close to the surface.

'Oh, he's been going on at us for days now. Every morning when we come to school he's there, waiting for us, calling us names, throwing stones at us. It's because we're evacuees – "vacees" he calls us. He doesn't like us because we're different from him.'

Hannah put her arm around the girl's shoulders and held her tight.

'Well, we're not all like him down here. Just ignore him, rotten bully that he is. I don't suppose he'll try much else for a while, not after today.'

Helen grinned back at her.

'I don't suppose so. Thanks to you and your friend!'

Peter suddenly stuck out his fist and seized Helen's arm. Energetically he shook her hand.

'I'm Peter,' he announced. 'Peter Longdale. It's good to meet you. That's Hannah Roberts and that latecomer over there is Jack Davies - his dad's the ARP warden! Very important man, he is!'

They went slowly into the school playground, Hannah and Helen helping the two younger girls.

'We haven't had many evacuees down here,' Hannah explained. 'I suppose it's because we're a bit too close to Swansea.'

Helen nodded.

'The only reason I'm here is because my mum's got family in Mumbles,' she said. 'I came here to stay with my Aunty Emily. It's not so hard for me. At least I know the people I'm staying with.'

She paused and nodded towards the two young girls.

'But for Ellie and Cathy it's awful. Herded onto a train, sent half way across the country and then living in strange houses with people they hardly know! Think how you'd feel if it was you.'

And then having to put up with bullies like Godfrey Scrivens, Hannah thought. That must be really nice for them!

'Nobody likes us,' cried one of the small girls. 'We haven't got any friends.'

Hannah ruffled her hair.

'Well you have now,' she said.

She smiled at the two youngsters and they seemed to grow in confidence.

'It was horrible,' cried the second girl. 'We didn't know where we were going. We stood for hours on Paddington Station. And they tied labels to our coats. Look.'

She held out her hand. Lying in the palm was a small brown label and a piece of string. On the label was her name and the destination – Swansea.

'She keeps it in her coat pocket,' said Helen, gently closing the girl's fingers around the precious label. 'It's all she's got to remind her of home.'

'We were on the train for hours,' the small girl continued. 'Hundreds of us, all crammed in together. And when we got to Swansea there were lots of men and women who came to stare at us. Most of them, all they wanted was servants and workers for their farms. We were lucky to come here.'

Hannah frowned. It sounded awful. She knew that she would have hated to be away from her mother, especially if there was danger. She glanced at the two girls.

'At play time I'll introduce you to my cousin Joan. She's about your age – she's probably in your class anyway. She'll be your friend, I promise.'

The two youngsters ran off happily to play hopscotch at the far side of the playground. Hannah smiled at Helen.

'As far as you're concerned, you've already got three new friends. Right?'

She indicated herself and the boys. Helen smiled, shyly.

'That would be nice,' she said.

Just then, the teacher called them in for the start of lessons. There was no bell – there had been no bells used in school since the beginning of the war. Bells were a signal for gas attacks.

Regretfully, the pupils filed into the grey school building, carrying their gas masks and packed lunches. Taking the gas masks with them wherever they went had become almost second nature now.

'That was really brave of you, Peter, back there,' said Hannah as they settled down at their desks. 'Godfrey Scrivens is twice your size.'

Peter shrugged. 'Not quite. And it was nothing – nothing you wouldn't have done if you'd got there first. We're fighting this war to get rid of bullies, aren't we? I suppose Hitler and Goering started off by bullying kids in the playground. Maybe if somebody had stood up to them then, we wouldn't be fighting today.'

He was so right, Hannah decided, but before she had time to say anything the teacher banged on her desk and lessons began. Mrs Stephens was old and grey-haired. She had retired from teaching several years before, but with so many of the young male teachers already serving in the armed forces had been called back to fill the gap.

'Right, children,' she called. 'This morning we are going to start with Maths. Get your books out.'

Hannah opened her desk and took out her arithmetic book. It was an ordinary exercise book but it had been cut in half – like most books in the class. It was all part of preserving valuable resources. She sighed and picked up her half-pencil: a hard day's work awaited her.

And then she glanced across to the far side of the classroom where Godfrey Scrivens sat in his normal place alongside the partition wall. He was staring at Peter, hatred alive and burning in his eyes. Whatever else had happened that morning, Peter Longdale had clearly made himself an enemy for life.

Even as she stared at him, Godfrey saw her and turned his head. His lip curled and he raised his left fist.

'You wait,' he mouthed.

Obviously she and Jack – and almost certainly Helen as well – were included in the threat. Hannah knew that there would be trouble ahead.

Chapter Three

It was four days before Christmas and Hannah and Helen were on Fairwood Common, collecting holly for decorations. The day was overcast and cold, a brisk wind from the west ensuring that the rain clouds moved swiftly on across Swansea and its foam-flecked bay.

'Let's try down here,' said Hannah. 'I reckon this part's been picked clean.'

She pointed towards a low depression in the ground. Beyond it the trees and undergrowth seemed particularly thick. Helen smiled and nodded to her friend.

'Okay. I'll leave these here.'

She put down her canvas bag, already half-full of holly, and pushed it into the foot of the hedge. Nobody would see it there and they would be able to pick it up later, after they had explored the valley in front of them.

'I'm glad school's over for the term,' Hannah said, easing her way through the brambles and bushes. 'I think I rather like the idea of having a longer holiday at Christmas. What about you?'

'Maybe,' said Helen, shrugging. 'It's great now but it does mean we'll have less time off in the summer.'

It had been another new idea from the government: by closing schools for longer in the winter months they would save valuable fuel like coal and oil.

Saving things had started to become really important – everything from food and drink to petrol.

Peter had sat and explained it one evening but Hannah wasn't sure that she had understood it all. Economics, as Peter had grandly called it, was clearly a very complex process. One thing she did understand, however, was that German U-boats were sinking large numbers of merchant ships. In a country where all of its oil and lots of its food had to come in by sea, that meant trouble – 'trouble with a capital T' as Peter had called it.

'Look,' called Helen, 'there's a big bunch over there.'

The holly was high up on an escarpment of rock but Hannah reckoned that with a bit of a climb they could easily reach their goal. If only Peter and Jack had agreed to come with them on the expedition, she thought. But they were too busy charting the war on Jack's *Daily Express* map. Jack had pinned it to the back of his bedroom door and he and Peter kept sticking little pins and bits of ribbon across the face of the chart.

Only last week, the German battleship *Graf Spee* had been sunk off South America. Jack had been beside himself with joy as he marked up the chart.

'See,' he'd crowed, 'they can't beat the Royal Navy. Three cruisers, that's all – *Ajax*, *Achilles* and *Exeter* – three cruisers, that's all it took. And they sank the greatest ship in the German navy.'

Hannah had been puzzled by that one. As far as she could work it out from the wireless reports and newspapers, the *Graf Spee* had blown herself up. She certainly hadn't been sunk by British guns. But then, a victory was a victory – and nothing much else seemed to be happening in the war.

'Come on,' said Helen, nudging her out of her reverie. 'Let's try for this holly.'

It took them only a few minutes to climb the rock and a short while later, Helen's scissors had done their work. Three fine bunches of holly, green and gleaming with red berries like flecks of blood, lay at the foot of the climb. Carefully, Hannah and Helen made their way down the rock.

'I reckon we should call it a day,' Hannah panted. 'There's enough here for you and me and there'll still be some left over to give to Peter and Jack. What do you think?'

Helen nodded, opened her mouth to speak and then froze.

'Voices!' she hissed.

Hannah glanced up the slope. Voices were, indeed, coming from the bushes that lined the top of the bank. The undergrowth was too thick to see anybody. Whoever was up there would not be able to see them either, but there was no mistaking that thin, weedy voice.

'Godfrey Scrivens!'

Since that morning in the school playground a few weeks before, Godfrey Scrivens had kept up a constant stream of abuse. By and large he left Peter alone. He had sensed something hard and unyielding in the boy and, for the time being at least, seemed to have decided that he was best avoided. Jack was clearly Peter's best friend, so there was nothing to be gained there. That left just Hannah and Helen.

For the past few weeks, the two girls had been the object of all Godfrey's anger and nastiness. It was mostly name-calling and threats of violence but it wasn't pleasant and it left them with a very uncomfortable feeling. Godfrey would just love this chance to catch them here on their own, miles away from anyone.

'Let's go,' said Helen. 'Quickly.'

There was genuine fear in her eyes.

'All right,' Hannah nodded. 'This way.'

She led Helen down the gully, moving deeper and deeper into the undergrowth. Soon the trees were arching overhead, blocking out their view of the sky. It was dark and spooky down here and the day seemed suddenly colder than ever.

'They're following us,' Helen hissed.

Hannah paused and listened carefully. From the gully behind them came the unmistakable sound of people moving quickly through the bushes. The voices were loud.

'I saw somebody, I'm sure I did!'

Hannah recognised Godfrey's voice and, despite herself, felt a sudden icy thrust of fear in her belly. It had been dangerous before, up at the opening of the gully or valley. Down here in the gloom, hidden from view and safety, the situation would be nothing short of desperate.

'We need to hide,' she said.

They were standing in a small clearing, surrounded by trees and rocks. Glancing urgently around, she saw a thick holly bush which clearly concealed a hollow or depression in the ground.

'Quick! In here.'

She pushed Helen down, under the bush, and threw herself in after her. She was not a moment too soon. Panting from fear and exhilaration she lay with her chin in the earth and saw Godfrey Scrivens and three boys force their way into the clearing. Godfrey was breathing heavily. His upper lip was drawn back and his prominent teeth stuck out like fangs against his mottled face.

The boys stood, gazing around, each of them searching the trees and undergrowth with their eager eyes. Finally, one of them shrugged.

'See?' he said. 'There's nobody here. I told you there wouldn't be. You were imagining things.'

Godfrey shook his head.

'I know I saw someone. It looked like Hannah Roberts. And if she was here, then you can bet that dirty 'vacee girl will be here with her.'

'So where are they?' demanded one of the others.

Godfrey stared around the clearing. For perhaps a minute he studied the scenery. His eyes lingered on the holly bush and Hannah swore he looked directly into her eyes. If she moved a muscle she knew that he would see them. She held her breath and prayed. Finally Godfrey looked away.

'Oh well,' he sighed. 'Perhaps I was wrong. Let's get back to the Common.'

The four boys turned on their heels and went out of the clearing. Hannah and Helen lay, motionless, until the noise of their progress had faded. For perhaps five minutes they waited, not moving and not speaking.

'Wow!' Helen whispered at last. 'I really thought we were done for then.'

The two girls smiled at each other and Helen stood up. Suddenly, the ground beneath her started to move.

'Hannah!' she screamed.

Hannah glanced around. Instantly she saw the problem. The earth behind the holly bush was fresh and soft. Their weight had started it moving, breaking away from the rock beneath – in effect, starting a mini avalanche. The bush hadn't just hidden a hollow in the ground. It had also hidden a steep slope.

'Stay still,' Hannah barked.

By now, however, Helen was terrified. She clawed at the earth, trying desperately to get back into the clearing but the more she scrabbled, the looser the earth became. Soon it was crumbling and sliding like the sand in an egg timer. And Helen was sliding with it.

Hannah lunged forward to grab her friend by the arm. The next second they were both catapulted backwards down the slope.

'Help!' screamed Helen.

'Oh no!'

As she fell Hannah had a sudden glimpse of

daylight above her and, for a brief moment, thought that her last moments had come. Tumbling and somersaulting like leaves in the wind, the two girls hurtled down the slope, crashing through bushes and bouncing off trees. A sudden pain in her knee told Hannah that she had hit a rock; then her coat tore with a resounding rip, a huge clod of earth hit her in the face and the whole world went suddenly black.

The next thing Hannah knew she was lying on her back at the foot of the slope. She could not have been unconscious long, she realised, as stray pieces of earth and grass were still clattering down from the hill above. For a few moments she lay and tried to breathe easily, then slowly began to check herself for bruises and breaks. Apart from a deep cut on her knee she seemed to be intact.

'Helen?' she said, turning around and looking for her friend.

'Over here.'

Helen was sitting, examining a graze on her arm, about six feet away. There were lumps of earth in her blonde hair but she was smiling with relief.

'How on earth did we get out of that?' she said. 'We should be dead.'

Hannah nodded and climbed gingerly to her feet. The slope down which they had fallen reared like a sheer cliff above them. Staring at it, Hannah couldn't help agreeing with Helen. They had been lucky.

'Tell you what,' she announced, 'we might have come down that hill but there's no way we can go back up it. It's far too steep.'

Helen glanced at her, panic shooting across her face.

'Where are we? Do you know?'

Hannah shook her head.

'I've got no idea. I've never been here before. It's some sort of valley, running parallel with the one up there – just fifty feet lower.'

She paused and looked around.

'Tell you what, let's try walking down here.'

She pointed down the valley to her left. The undergrowth seemed to be a little less thick down there – maybe there was a way out. Helen nodded and, together, the girls began to walk.

Despite everything, Hannah could not stop grinning. It had been so exciting – hiding from Godfrey Scrivens, the fall down the hill. In fact it had almost been like taking part in the war. She could hardly wait until she saw Peter and Jack again. What a story she would have to tell them.

For five minutes they walked. And all the time Hannah was conscious of something strange. Something was niggling away at the back of her mind. Suddenly, she realised what it was.

'Look,' she said, coming to a halt and grabbing at Helen's arm. 'This is a track, a pathway. Somebody's been this way before. Several times.'

She pointed at the ground. In the centre of the valley, where they were walking, the grass lay flattened and low where feet had formed it into a narrow path.

'Who made it, do you think? Godfrey?'

Hannah shrugged. 'I don't know. But if there's a

38

track then there's got to be a way out. Come on. At least it proves we're heading in the right direction.'

They went on, carefully keeping to the path.

'Having fun?' asked Hannah.

Helen glanced across and tried to smile. She failed dismally. 'Fun isn't exactly the word I'd use.'

'It's got to be more interesting than walking around Lambeth. I mean, all you get there are streets and concrete.'

Helen looked up sharply.

'We do have the occasional park, you know. We may not have hills to fall down but it doesn't make Lambeth any less exciting.'

She fell silent. Hannah said nothing and waited for her friend to speak again.

'I do like it down here – now that I've met you and the boys. But it's still not home, is it? Lambeth is where I belong, it's where I live. You wouldn't like to be sent away from your mum, not knowing what's happening to her. It's the same with my parents. I worry about them all the time.'

Hannah took the girl's arm and pulled her tight.

'Don't, Helen. Don't worry. There hasn't been an air raid on London yet. I shouldn't think there ever will be, either.'

They stared at each other. They both knew that the government had expected raids before this. After all, it was enemy dive bombs that had destroyed the Polish armies so quickly and completely. But at the moment, everything was unnaturally calm.

'If there are to be no raids,' said Helen, suddenly,

'then maybe I should go home. After all, the only reason I'm here is to avoid the bombing.'

Hannah shook her head.

'Not yet, surely? Leave it till the Spring. My mum says it'll be over by then, anyway.'

They went on down the path. Bordered by tall trees and dense bushes, they were now walking in a dark avenue, cut off from the outside world. Soon, however, the track crested a ridge and began to run downhill. At this point they seemed to be suddenly standing above the trees. And then, ahead, Hannah saw a glistening ribbon of silver light. It was the sea.

'I'm still not sure where we are,' she smiled, 'but with the sea over there I'll be able to work it out. If we head for the sea I reckon we'll be all right.'

'Come on, then,' said Helen. 'Let's go home.'

Before they could move, a voice suddenly rang out. It was tremulous and cracked but even when they first heard it the two girls knew that it was not directed at them. Perhaps more importantly the voice was singing – singing in a foreign language.

'What's that?' whispered Helen, afraid once more.

Hannah narrowed her eyes and listened. The voice seemed to be coming from all around them, echoing and bouncing off the trees.

> *Stille Nacht, heilige Nacht,*
> *Alles schläft, einsam wacht*
> *Nur das traute, hochheilige Paar.'*

Hannah and Helen stood, frozen with fear, as a small slight figure emerged from the bushes, about a hundred yards in front of them. He was dressed in a long grey overcoat and a battered felt hat, pulled down over his eyes. Head bent, the man shuffled along, singing to himself, and disappeared under the shadow of the trees.

'Who was that?' asked Helen. 'And what language was he speaking?'

Hannah's mind was working feverishly. The man had not seen them. He had gone happily down the track but his voice still echoed back up the hill towards them.

'Stille Nacht, heilige Nacht,
Alles schläft, einsam wacht.'

Desperately Hannah grabbed at Helen's arm.

'I don't know who he was,' she said, 'but that language was German. He was singing a Christmas Carol – 'Silent Night' – in German.'

Fear had gathered like a fist in her windpipe. Yet despite the fear, Hannah knew that she had to follow the man, whoever he was.

'Come on,' she said.

Grabbing at Helen's arm, she set off down the track, in pursuit of the stranger. Helen tried pulling back but it was no use. Helpless and afraid, she found herself dragged headlong in Hannah's wake.

'Hannah, stop,' she protested, 'please stop. We shouldn't be doing this. It could be dangerous. We don't know who that man is – he could be a murderer or an escaped convict. Please Hannah, let's stop.'

Hannah ignored her and marched powerfully down the track. A hundred yards on, almost hidden from view amongst the bushes, they came across a small black hut. It was old and battered, made of corrugated iron and wood and was set back amongst the bushes at the side of the path. There was no sign of the strange man but a thin stream of smoke was escaping from a tin can set into the roof – obviously a makeshift chimney.

'Look,' said Hannah, 'there's a light.'

She pointed to a window in the side of the hut. A yellow glow, bright as a bush fire, shone in the gloom of the avenue. Surprised that she was capable of rational thought, Hannah instinctively realised that the hut was almost invisible to view – unless, like them, you literally fell on top of it. At the same time, however, from the wide front window there was a perfect and uncluttered view of the sea and the Bristol Channel.

Hannah inched forward to get a better look. The sea lay only a few hundred yards away, framed by the dark mass of trees and bushes on either side of the avenue. Even as she stared, a sleek destroyer came charging up the Channel, smoke billowing from its funnels and white spray arching up from its bows. Behind it came the bulky shapes of merchant ships. A convoy was heading for Swansea or Cardiff.

'What a great place for a spy,' she hissed, turning urgently to her friend. 'If anybody wanted to count the ships out there in the channel this would be the perfect spot.'

42

'A spy?' whispered Helen. 'You think he's a spy?'

For weeks now the papers had been full of scare stories about spies and fifth columnists. There were hundreds of them, Hannah had read, all across Britain, just waiting for the chance to help enemy paratroopers land or to radio military secrets back to Germany. She stared at Helen, eyes wide with excitement.

'Well, this place is miles from anywhere. I bet nobody even knows it's here – apart from that man in there. It's the ideal spot for a spy to live.'

Helen was terrified. She clutched at Hannah's arm and tried, desperately, to pull her away.

'Come on, let's get out of here.'

Hannah shook her head. 'We've got to look inside.'

She gestured towards the hut on the other side of the avenue. Helen was rooted to the spot, however, her legs trembling and tears gathering at the corner of her eyes. Nothing on God's earth would make her move now. Hannah shrugged.

'Stay here, then,' she said. 'I'll go.'

She inched forward, walking on tiptoe across the clearing. In less than a minute she had reached the wall of the hut and turned to wave to Helen. Then she moved carefully to the side window. The glass was cracked and dirty but by pushing her face close up against it Hannah was able to see inside.

The man was sitting, crouched over a fire, cooking something that looked like stew in an old billycan. Tendrils of grey smoke filled the hut. Like long fingers of mist or fog, the smoke wreathed around the strange man's head. There was a camp bed pushed up against the wall beneath the window and an oil lamp stood on the floor, casting its yellow glow across the room and out into the woods.

'Hannah! Please come back.'

Helen was standing in the darkness of the avenue, hissing and waving, urging her to come away from the hut. Hannah gestured for her to keep quiet and turned back to the window. Something on the far wall had caught her attention – a large picture or photograph. She stared at it and gasped. It was Adolf Hitler – Hitler standing in the back of an open car, his arm raised in the Nazi salute. All around him the faces of his adoring public were raised up in ecstasy.

'Oh, my God,' Hannah gasped.

At that moment, the man inside the hut turned towards the window and their eye met. He had a thick moustache, flecked with grey and his eyes, bloodshot and ugly, bored into Hannah's soul.

She fell back from the window and screamed. Then she ran. Grabbing Helen's arm, she tore off down the path, heading blindly towards the sea.

'What was it?' Helen demanded as they fled. 'What did you see, Hannah? What was it?'

Hannah did not reply. All her breath and energy sent her hurtling down the path, dragging Helen in her wake. Behind them, in the darkness of the wood, the tiny hut stood silent and still.

Chapter Four

'Where was this place exactly?' asked Peter.

It was later that same afternoon and they were sitting in Conti's Café on the seafront. To their right, Mumbles Pier was deserted, a gaunt outline in the winter sunshine. Behind them, the hiss of Mr Conti's silver coffee machine sounded like an exploding volcano in the silent room. They were the only customers in the café.

'Four coffees,' said Mr Conti, leaning across the table and placing the cups in front of each of them in turn. 'Made especially for you.'

Hannah liked the way he managed to carry four cups and saucers at the same time. She had tried it once, in the kitchen at home, but all she succeeded in doing was dropping all four.

'Thanks, Mr Conti,' said Peter.

The café owner smiled at them. His old eyes, watery and grey, were full of kindness. Today, however, there was also sadness in his manner.

'Are you all right, Mr Conti?' asked Hannah

'Enjoy the coffees,' he shrugged. 'I don't know how much longer I'll be able to serve you with them.'

'What do you mean, Mr Conti?'

He shrugged and spread his arms. It was a very Italian gesture, somehow. Mr Conti had lived most of his life in Wales, but in his gestures and his accent he remained very much an Italian.

'Coffee,' he said. 'It is getting very difficult to buy coffee. These damned Germans and their submarines.'

'They're called U-boats, Mr Conti,' said Jack.

The old man sniffed. 'Submarines, U-boats? Whatever. They are causing many problems for poor people like me.'

He looked as if he might cry, Hannah thought. She smiled up at him.

'How is your family, Mr Conti?'

The old man was not to be denied his misery, however. He shrugged and inclined his head two or three times.

'Mrs Conti, she's taking it badly, this war. She was supposed to go to Rimini last September, to see her family. There aren't many of them left alive, you know. None of us getting any younger. But this war, these Germans and their submarines!'

He wandered away, mumbling to himself and began to sort through the spoons and ice cream dishes on his counter. Hannah stared at him until Peter's voice broke in on her thoughts and dragged her back to the present.

'Come on, then, Hannah, where was this hut?'

She exchanged quick glances with Helen.

'We don't know, exactly,' she said. 'I told you, we fell down the bank, into a sort of hidden valley. When we came out – after we'd seen the man – we were on the coast, somewhere beyond Langland Bay. I don't know where it is exactly but we could take you there, couldn't we, Helen?'

Helen's head came up sharply in alarm. The idea of going back to that hut in the woods did not appeal to her very much. But she nodded her head and tried her best to smile.

'Yes, I suppose we could.'

'Come on, then,' said Jack. 'Let's go and find this strange old man of yours.'

He was clearly excited and intrigued. In his mind there was no doubt about it. The man was a spy and he needed to be captured before he could do any real damage. Jack had been keen to get involved in the war for ages. This was his big chance.

They finished their coffees and went out of the café, waving their goodbyes to Mr Conti. Already it was getting dark and the wind from across the bay was chilling.

'Can't we leave it until tomorrow?' asked Helen.

Peter shook his head.

'Not if he saw you. If he is actually a spy, he might have made a run for it. We need to check it out now, this afternoon.'

He paused and gazed up at the darkening sky.

'Or rather, tonight.'

Jack nodded. There was a gleam in his eyes and he was desperately keen for action.

'Then we can catch him.'

Peter shook his head and sighed. 'No, Jack. We aren't going to catch anybody. We're just going to check it out. Then we'll report to my father. He can do the catching.'

Jack wasn't convinced, however.

'Why your dad? He was showing a light. That's ARP business. My dad's the ARP warden.'

Peter sighed again. 'Then we'll tell both of them. Now come on, time's getting short.'

They went quickly along the road on their bicycles, pedalling furiously up the hill away from the seafront. Within minutes, Mumbles lay well behind them. Hannah took the lead, directing them along the coast towards the place where she and Helen had eventually emerged from the hidden valley.

After a while they left their bikes leaning up against the hedge and went on by foot. Peter pulled his cycle lamp off the handlebars of his bike and dropped it into his pocket, shrugging as he did so.

'We'll probably need some light in a little while,' he said.

'It's getting really dark,' Helen whispered. 'We'll never find the place now.'

Nobody answered and they ploughed on in the gathering gloom. At last, however, Hannah came to a halt. The others pulled up behind her.

'It's just here. Isn't it, Helen?'

She pointed at the trees on their right. Helen nodded. Jack and Peter peered at the undergrowth and then, eventually, relaxed as they picked out the entrance to the valley. In this light it looked like nothing more than a darker shade of black.

'It's like a tunnel,' breathed Jack. 'You'd never know it was there unless you fell into it.'

Peter stared at the entrance to the valley, then out

over the channel. He seemed to be studying the landscape.

'Well?'

'Wait a minute,' Peter said.

He swung towards Hannah and waved his arm toward the sea.

'Great view. Like looking down a telescope.'

Hannah nodded. That was exactly what she felt. And the more she thought about it, the more convinced she became – that man in the hut just had to be a spy.

'Come on, then,' said Peter.

Carefully, they inched up the slope and into the avenue of trees. Peter pulled out his bike lamp and switched it on. The beam had been restricted by sticking pieces of dark tape across the lens in order to comply with blackout precautions. The light was dim but at least it meant that they could see where they were going.

It was eerie here in the avenue of trees, long shadows seeming to reach out at them from the darkness. Even to Hannah, determined as she was to discover the truth, it was as if black-coated bodies lay hidden behind every tree, carefully watching their progress, preparing to jump out and grab them as they passed.

'I don't like this,' whispered Helen. 'I'm scared.'

'You'll be okay,' breathed Jack.

His voice, Hannah noticed, was shaking. He seemed to have lost a lot of his confidence and was continually glancing around in the darkness. The thought of what could be waiting up ahead did not sit easily with any of them.

'The hut's about a hundred yards up there,' Hannah said at last.

The path had begun to rise steeply. At the top of it, a bright yellow light shone out across the trees.

'I don't care if he is a spy or not,' muttered Jack. 'Wait till my dad knows about this. Showing lights at night! He'll have the bloke inside before you can say 'Jack Robinson'.'

'Quietly now,' hissed Peter.

They tiptoed up the path, coming to a halt twenty yards short of the hut. All of them were breathing heavily.

'Listen!' said Helen.

From inside the hut came the sound of voices.

'He's talking to someone,' said Hannah. 'That means there's two of them in there. Or maybe even more.'

'Stay here,' said Peter. 'I'm going to take a look.'

He inched forward while Hannah glanced urgently around. The other two clearly had no intention of moving but she knew that she had to see what was going on inside the hut. She was blowed if she was going to let Peter do it all on his own. Moving quickly, she caught up with him before he had got even halfway to the hut. He glanced at her as she joined him.

'Don't say a word,' she whispered.

Peter shook his head and smiled.

'I wasn't going to.'

They eased up to the window and carefully peered

inside. Despite herself, Hannah immediately started to giggle and Peter elbowed her, hard in the ribs.

Inside the hut the strange man was sitting on his bed. His eyes were closed and he was contentedly sucking at a short stumpy pipe. On a table in the corner, a wireless was playing loudly. Every so often the man chortled and muttered to himself or shouted out a comment or a response to what he had heard. There was nobody else in the room.

'A wireless,' Peter exclaimed. 'It's just a wireless. Somebody's talking on the wireless.'

'That's not just somebody,' Hannah whispered, 'that's Lord Haw Haw.'

For two minutes they watched and listened. It was indeed Lord Haw Haw. You couldn't mistake those false, plummy tones. William Joyce was an Englishman who had been broadcasting from Hamburg since the war began. The broadcasts were meant to be German propaganda, messages from Hitler and the other Nazi leaders that were designed to dent people's morale. Britons, however, simply laughed at the man's accent and appeals for peace. The government had banned people from listening to Lord Haw Haw, as he had soon been dubbed, but everyone switched him on, regardless of regulations.

'Look!' whispered Hannah. 'There's the picture of Hitler on the wall. Just like I told you.'

The image of the Führer was unmistakable. They had seen enough. Peter and Hannah backed away from the window and rejoined the others further down the track.

'Well?' asked Jack.

Peter shrugged.

'He's in there, all right. There's nobody with him – it was just the wireless. He was listening to Lord Haw Haw.'

He smiled at Helen and nudged her with his shoulder, trying hard to lighten the atmosphere.

'Seems like you and Hannah didn't frighten him away after all.'

Helen gazed at him, wide-eyed.

'So, do you think he's a spy?'

Jack snorted and spun around to face them. His eyes were shining in the darkness and he seemed to have recovered a little of his enthusiasm for the adventure.

'Of course he's a spy. He was listening to Lord Haw Haw, wasn't he? He's got a picture of Hitler on his wall. And he was showing a light – a light that's invisible to anybody unless they're out at sea. I bet he was signalling to a U-boat in the channel. He's a spy all right.'

They stood and considered it. The weight of evidence did seem particularly strong. At last Peter shrugged.

'We need to find help. Somebody's got to stay, just to make sure he doesn't escape. And somebody will have to go back and bring some adults out here to deal with him.'

He nodded towards the hut and its hidden occupant. Nobody spoke. Ten seconds passed.

'I'll go,' said Helen.

Hannah smiled at her friend, knowing how much courage the offer had taken. Helen hated the dark. To be alone in the night, out in strange countryside, would not have been something she relished.

'I'll go too,' said Jack suddenly. 'Helen shouldn't be on her own at night. And I can explain it all to my father'

There was no response. Hannah could hear him breathing, waiting for approval from her and Peter. They said nothing.

'Let me have your torch,' Jack said eventually. 'We'll need it to see where we're going.'

Peter held out the lamp. Almost without a pause, Jack took it and started back down the track to the sea. With a faint grin, Helen turned and followed him.

'Oh, Jack?' Peter called softly. 'My father as well as yours. Okay?'

Jack waved. 'Of course. The more the merrier, I say.'

Within seconds, he and Helen were lost to view.

*   *   *

'How much longer, do you think?'

Peter and Hannah were waiting in the bushes a few hundred yards beyond the hut. For over an hour they had been sitting there, keeping their eyes fixed firmly on the stream of yellow light that poured from the window.

'I don't know,' Peter shrugged. 'My dad should be home by now. If not, my mum will tell Jack where to find him. Another hour, perhaps?'

They lapsed into silence. After a while Hannah felt her eyes beginning to close. It wasn't so bad, this darkness, once you got used to it, once your eyes and senses had become accustomed to the gloom. It was almost reassuring, she felt – at least, as long as someone like Peter was there to keep her company. Her head fell sideways onto his shoulder and she slept. How long she was asleep, Hannah did not know but suddenly she sensed a new tension in Peter alongside her. Instantly she was awake.

'What is it?'

Peter was pointing towards the hut.

'Look. He's signalling to someone.'

Hannah peered across the clearing. The light was still showing but now it was no longer a steady glow. Now it was flickering. On, off, on, off, went the light. The man inside was obviously holding his lamp to the window and passing something across in front of the beam.

'So he is a spy!' Hannah exclaimed. 'I knew it. The minute I heard him speaking German I guessed he was up to no good. Now he's making signals to his accomplice. Do you think it's a U-boat?'

Peter climbed carefully but purposefully to his feet.

'We've got to stop him,' he said. 'There could be boatloads of Germans landing here in a few minutes.'

He was halfway across the clearing when the sound of hammering suddenly began inside the hut. The flickering yellow beam vanished. All they could now see was a small square of light from the side window.

'What's happened?' asked Hannah.

Peter shrugged. He stood in the centre of the clearing, unsure whether to go on or come back to the shadows.

'What was that hammering?'

They listened, carefully. No more noise came from inside the hut and there was no more signalling. More importantly, there were no sounds of enemy troops on the path and beach below. Everything was quiet. Peter slipped back into the bushes and sat alongside Hannah once more.

'That was really strange. Who was he signalling to? And that banging – it sounded like he was making something. Or mending it.'

'Perhaps he was fixing his radio,' said Hannah.

'With a hammer?'

Peter stared at her and they laughed. Put like that, it did sound pretty stupid.

For another hour they waited in the bushes, watching the hut and listening intently for any sounds that might signal trouble – or the arrival of reinforcements.

It was a relief to finally hear the sound of hushed voices and the steady tramp of feet coming up the hill towards them. Hannah frowned and hoped that the spy was still listening to his wireless. Otherwise, there would be only an empty hut to greet the newcomers.

'Peter?'

It was Jack, calling out in a hushed whisper. He flashed the torch and Peter and Hannah slipped out of the bushes. Hannah recognised the tall shape of PC Longdale in his uniform, and behind him stood the short, squat figure of Mr Davies. Jack had been as good as his word and informed both of them.

'Has he moved?' asked PC Longdale, placing one hand on his son's shoulder and gesturing towards the hut with the other.

Peter shook his head.

'No, but he was signalling just now. He kept flashing a light. On and off it went, for three or four minutes. I don't know morse code but my guess is he was signalling to somebody out at sea.'

'Was he now?' muttered Mr Davies. 'Serious problem, showing lights during the blackout. Come on then, Mr Longdale, let's go and see what we've got.'

PC Longdale looked up and straightened his tunic. He turned to Peter and carefully, deliberately, pointed his finger.

'You stay here. All of you. You've done quite enough as it is, charging across the countryside, putting yourselves in all sorts of danger. Leave this to us. Understand?'

He glanced at the ARP man and nodded. Together with Mr Davies, he strode across the clearing. There was a loud bang and the next second the yellow beam of light shot across the woodland once more.

Hannah heard the policeman's voice – 'Now, then, what do we have here?' – and then the door closed behind him.

Hannah and the others stood quietly in the dark.

None of them felt inclined to speak, each of them straining hard to catch something, anything, that was being said inside the hut.

For ten minutes they stood there. Finally, however, the hut door opened and three men came out. Without even a backward glance, Mr Davies and the spy went down the path and disappeared into the night. PC Longdale gazed after them, then walked over to the four youngsters.

'So much for your spy,' he grinned.

Hannah could barely contain herself.

'You mean he wasn't a spy, not a fifth columnist?'

PC Longdale shook his head. Then he began to laugh. His voice echoed around the clearing, the laughter reverberating off the trees. Hannah stared at him, not understanding.

'Tell us, Mr Longdale. Please?'

'What's so funny, Dad?' asked Peter.

The policeman wiped his eyes and drew himself up to his full height. Still chuckling, he led them across the clearing and into the hut.

'He wasn't a spy,' he said, 'just a harmless old man. His name is Mr Williamson and he comes from Llanelli, just down the coast. He's been living out here ever since his wife died back in the summer. He just wanted to be alone.'

'But the signalling? He was . . .'

PC Longdale held up his hand, stopping his son in his tracks. He turned and pointed towards the window.

'His curtain – not really a blackout curtain, just a

bit of cloth – had come loose. It was flapping in the wind. Until he took a hammer and a couple of nails. And fixed it.'

He stared at the bed. A small hammer and three nails lay on the pillow.

'What about the singing?' Hannah said suddenly. 'The German Christmas carol. We heard him, didn't we, Helen?'

Helen nodded vigorously.

'In German,' she said. 'He was singing in German. Honestly.'

PC Longdale smiled and nodded his head.

'I'm sure he was. His wife was Austrian. "Silent Night" is an Austrian carol. It was what the Germans sang to our soldiers during the Christmas truce back in 1914. Mr Williamson says his wife taught it to him years ago. It's always been a favourite of his.'

'And the wireless? Listening to Lord Haw Haw?'

The policeman sat down on the bed and stared at Hannah. Then he took off his helmet and laid it down alongside him.

'Listening to poor old William Joyce? Don't you? I know I do. Half the country listens to him every night.' He looked up sharply. 'Of course, you shouldn't. Or at least you shouldn't admit to it. But, let's be honest, Lord Haw Haw is the funniest thing on the wireless at the moment.'

He was right, Hannah decided. Everybody she knew tuned into Lord Haw Haw. She grinned. What fools they had been! And then she glanced across the room. The photograph of Adolf Hitler was still there, pinned to the far wall. She opened her mouth to speak but PC Longdale had followed her gaze and was ready for her.

'Oh that,' he smiled. 'It's covering up a crack in the wall. Best use I can think of for the Führer. If you look a little closer, Hannah, you'll see the crack in the wood behind the photo. And old Adolf isn't the only one either.'

He pointed at the walls of the hut. All over the wood surfaces there were photographs, most of them having been ripped out of magazines and newspapers. All of them covered cracks or holes in the woodwork. Hannah glanced quickly around and amongst the others recognised Laurel and Hardy, Prime Minister Chamberlain and even the Pope.

'Quite a gallery,' said PC Longdale. 'But, then, he didn't care what they showed. He only wanted them to keep out the wind.'

He stood up and carefully put on his helmet. He smiled at Hannah and Helen.

'Just a word, girls. If he had been a spy, he'd hardly have been likely to put a photograph of the Führer on the wall, would he?'

Hannah blushed and Helen giggled. They'd had eyes only for Hitler; hadn't even noticed the other pictures. But what the policeman had said made a lot of sense, Hannah decided. Next time, they would think before acting.

'Right,' said PC Longdale, 'let's see about getting you four home.'

He put out the light and ushered them out. Then he

locked the door of the hut and set off down the track towards the sea. The moon had risen and there was a beautiful silver glow across the water.

'Bombers' moon,' said the policemen.

'Sorry?'

'Bombers' moon. It's so light you'd have to be blind not to see your target tonight – blackout or no blackout.'

Hannah felt Helen shiver alongside her and knew that it was time to change the subject.

'What's going to happen to the old man? Mr Williamson?'

'Oh, he'll be all right,' said PC Longdale. 'He hasn't done anything really wrong. Mr Davies has taken him along to the Clearing Station. They'll fix him up with something – something a lot better than a draughty old hut in the woods. They'll probably get him lodgings, a place where somebody can look after him, cook his meals, that type of thing. He'll be a lot happier there.'

Maybe, thought Hannah, but the old man had chosen to live by himself in the woods. He must be grieving for his wife, looking for peace and quiet. It was what he had wanted and surely nobody had a right to intrude on that? As if he could sense her thoughts, the policeman glanced across and took her gently by the arm.

'It's war time, Hannah. He couldn't be left there, alone, like that. He was a danger to himself and a risk to others, showing lights like he did. If a U-boat had been lying off shore it would have been a disaster – it would have brought the bombers here like bees round a honey pot.'

Despite everything, Hannah knew he was right. It was the war, she thought, and wondered if things could ever get much worse. She felt terribly tired, all of a sudden, and knew that tonight she would sleep like a log.

Chapter Five

Christmas was over and the adventure of 'the spy who wasn't' – as Peter had christened the affair – was consigned to memory. Soon it was back to school and, with the phoney war dragging on, the pattern of life continued much as normal. Lessons were as boring and as necessary as ever, although, to be fair, Mrs Stephens did try to enliven things whenever she could. Following the course of the war was just one of her tactics.

One morning, as the class pored over its history books, there was a knock on the door and the caretaker staggered into the room. He was dragging a large wooden screen behind him.

'Just here, Mr Jones,' said the teacher, pointing to an open space next to her desk.

They watched as the caretaker set up the screen. It was tall and heavy and stood like a wardrobe at the front of the classroom.

'We'll put a map on here,' Mrs Stephens declared, pointing to the panels on the left side of the screen. 'Whenever anything happens – anything of note, that is – we'll stick in a coloured pin. Then we can learn about the place and its history. And we can write about it and put our essays on this side.'

She rested her finger on the other part of the screen. Jack snorted. He was unimpressed. His own battle map had soon been abandoned, once he had realised that little or nothing was happening on the war front.

'Don't worry, Jack.' Mrs Stephens said. 'Things will hot up sooner or later. Maybe then you'll wish they hadn't.'

Jack said nothing but Hannah knew that he was thinking about his brother with the BEF in France.

*   *   *

One Saturday in early April, Hannah called for Helen at her aunt's house. They were due to meet Peter and Jack at Conti's Café in half an hour. When Hannah arrived, Helen and her aunt, Mrs Livingstone, were in the kitchen, listening to the wireless.

'Come in, Hannah,' said Mrs Livingstone. 'I've been meaning to thank you for your kindness to Ellie and Cathy, Helen's little friends. They're so much happier since your cousin took them under her wing.'

Hannah smiled and shook her head.

'It was nothing, Mrs Livingstone, nothing at all.'

Helen indicated that she should sit alongside her.

'There's something happening in Norway,' she said, gesturing towards the wireless set. 'Something to do with ships in a place called Narvik.'

Together, they sat and listened for a while but it wasn't really all that interesting. They put on their coats and set off for the seafront.

'Make sure you wear your hat, Helen,' called Mrs Livingstone as they went down the front path. 'You, too, Hannah. It might seem sunny but it's still cold out there.'

The two girls pulled on their woollen hats; items

of clothing they had knitted at school, along with socks and gloves for the soldiers in France. As soon as they turned the corner, however, they happily dragged off the hats and stuffed them into their pockets. Hannah shook out her jet-black hair and ran her fingers through the curls.

'Can't stand anything on my head,' she declared. 'I like to feel the wind in my hair.'

They went down the street and, after a few minutes, came out on the seafront. The breeze down here was fresher and both girls pulled their coats tight. The hated hats stayed in their pockets, however.

Almost immediately, Hannah picked out the shape of Jack Davies standing on the opposite side of the road. Yet it really wasn't Jack who caught her attention. Leaning on the rail alongside him was a tall, well-built man in the khaki uniform of a soldier. He stood casually, one foot up on the railing and his beret thrust through the epaulette on his left shoulder. Hannah recognised him immediately, even though he seemed to have grown a couple of feet since she had last seen him six months ago.

'Who's that?' asked Helen, following her friend's gaze.

'That's Jack's brother, Tommy. He must have come home from France.'

They crossed the road and made their way up the pavement towards their friend. Jack saw them coming and turned to greet them, smiling broadly. He was clearly proud of his big brother and pleased to be able to show him off at last.

'Look,' he called, 'look. Tommy's home on leave.'

Jack could barely keep still, his excitement forcing him to bob from foot to foot like a circus clown. He clutched at Hannah's arm, then turned to face his brother.

'Tommy, look, it's Hannah! You remember Hannah, don't you? And this is Helen. She's an evacuee from London. This is my brother, Helen. He's a lance corporal.'

Tommy took his foot off the rail and half turned towards them. He smiled, distantly.

'It's lance bombardier, Jack. I'm in the artillery – they call us bombardiers in the artillery, not corporals. Hello there, Hannah. Where's your friend Peter?'

Hannah shrugged and pointed back over her shoulder.

'Oh, he's coming. We were supposed to meet him and Jack in the café ten minutes ago.'

Tommy nodded and turned back towards the sea. He pulled a packet of Woodbines from his tunic and lit a cigarette, casually tossing the dead match over the rail onto the beach.

'Have you heard the news?' Hannah asked, turning towards Jack.

'No. What's happened?'

'I'm not sure exactly. But I think it was a battle in Norway. I didn't hear all of it. It was something about British destroyers and a place – a fjord, I think – called Narvik. It sounded like a big action was going on.'

Tommy turned suddenly towards them.

'Norway's a sideshow,' he said. 'We won't hold Jerry there. We're not equipped or trained to fight in the snow. Jerry is. We'll pull out of Norway in a week or so. It's a side show, believe me.'

He paused and stared over Hannah's shoulder. His eyes widened as he flicked his half-smoked cigarette away.

'There's your friend Peter,' he said, 'coming now.'

Jack pulled urgently at his brother's arm, keen to know more. What had Tommy meant about a sideshow, he demanded.

'A sideshow,' Tommy smiled, 'something that doesn't really matter. No, France and Belgium – that's where this war will be won or lost. Take my word for it. Hello, Peter.'

Peter Longdale had joined them. He smiled, pleased that Tommy had remembered his name, and held out his arm.

'How's your sister Mary?' Tommy asked, shaking Peter by the hand.

Peter shrugged. 'She was fine when I left home five minutes ago. Sitting in the kitchen, darning socks.'

'So she's there now?'

'I suppose so. She wasn't planning on going anywhere.'

Tommy moved to the pavement edge. He paused as a truck full of soldiers rumbled past, the bored faces of the men in the back gazing mournfully out. Jack made to follow his brother.

'No, Jack,' said Tommy, holding up his hand. 'You stay here with your friends.'

Jack was crestfallen. He had desperately wanted to parade round town with his brother, showing him off to everyone they met.

'We'll go for a walk later,' Tommy smiled, darting quickly across the road in front of a second truck full of soldiers. 'I promise.'

On the far side he turned and waved. Then he was gone, walking swiftly up the road out of sight.

Jack turned to face his friends, trying hard to smile.

'Shall we go to Conti's?'

They nodded and set off along the seafront. Tiny waves were breaking on the beach and the wind across the bay had a knife-sharp edge to it. Yet the sun shone and there was hardly a cloud in the sky.

'When did Tommy come home?' asked Peter.

Almost immediately, Jack begun to cheer up – just to talk about his brother made him feel better.

'Late last night. He had to bring some gun parts back to his regiment's base in Aldershot. They won't be repaired for a few days so he was given a 48-hour pass. He's got to be in London again by tomorrow night. Then he's going back to France.'

They settled themselves at their usual table by the window of the café and ordered their drinks from Mr Conti. The old Italian smiled shyly at them but did not speak. Like so many people these days he seemed to have a lot on his mind. For ten minutes the friends sat talking, sipping at their drinks. Then Hannah glanced up, startled.

'Look,' she said. 'There's Tommy over there. And isn't that Mary with him?'

Across the road, Tommy and Mary, Peter's beautiful sister, were walking, arm in arm. Even from this distance it was clear that they had eyes only for each other.

'So that's why he was asking about Mary,' whistled Peter, sitting back in his chair and laying his hands flat on the tabletop. 'Don't they make a lovely couple!'

Hannah and Helen laughed but Jack, they noticed, was strangely quiet.

'I didn't know Tommy and Mary were going out together,' said Hannah. 'I wonder how long that's been going on?'

Peter shrugged his shoulders.

'Can't say I knew much about it either. What about you, Jack?'

The smaller boy shook his head and said nothing. Suddenly Peter leaned across the table and punched Jack lightly on the arm.

'Tell you what, though,' he grinned. 'I reckon this makes us relatives. Or it will do soon!'

Jack snorted. Clearly he did not find the situation as amusing as Peter. He had wanted his brother to himself for the short time he was at home.

'Oh shut up, Peter,' he snorted, suddenly.

He pushed himself to his feet and stormed out of the door. The other three stared, dumbfounded, at his retreating back. Finally, however, Peter spoke.

'It's certainly starting to be one hell of a war,' he declared.

*   *   *

It wasn't long before things turned much worse. Hannah would remember the date for the rest of her life – 10th May. That morning she woke early and went downstairs to find her mother with her head close up to the wireless set.

'It's started,' said Mrs Roberts as Hannah came in through the kitchen door. 'The Germans have attacked Belgium and Holland. They're trying to get round the Maginot Line into France.'

Hannah felt a sudden pang, a real and livid pain in her belly. Jack's brother had said it would happen in Belgium and France. It seemed like he was right.

'They're not telling us much on the wireless,' said Mrs Roberts. 'All they seem to be saying is that the Germans have attacked on a broad front – whatever that might mean.'

They listened for a while to Alvar Lidell's plush and plummy voice on the wireless. Then, while her mother prepared breakfast, Hannah laid the table and wondered about Jack's brother. Tommy would probably be in action at this very moment, she thought, and decided she would go and call for Jack so that they could walk to school together.

When she arrived at his house, Jack was sitting with his parents, listening to the wireless.

'They're giving broadcasts every hour,' Jack whispered as Hannah sat alongside him. 'At the moment it's all music. Listen to that – Flannagan and Allan. "We're going to hang out the washing on the Siegfried Line". What a joke that is. We're waiting for the next announcement.'

There was a knock at the door and Peter and Helen joined them.

'I don't know,' said Jack's father, trying hard to force a grin, 'this place is as busy as Woolworths.'

The following week – and for the next few weeks after that – Mrs Stephens' war map was full of little red pins and bits of coloured cotton. The German advance had been rapid, a Blitzkrieg as Mrs Stephens called it. And the Allied troops seemed to have no answer to the tactic.

'The BEF has fallen back,' said the teacher, pointing to an area on the coast. 'With the French armies crumbling all around them, they've had no option but to retreat. They'll probably make a stand here.'

Once more her finger jabbed into the map. The children who were clustered around the screen strained hard to read the name.

'Dunkirk,' said Peter. 'It's called Dunkirk.'

'Swot,' grumbled Godfrey Scrivens who was standing on the other side of the group. 'Trust him to know the name.'

Peter shook his head and stared, disdainfully, at the class bully.

'I just listen to the news occasionally,' he said. 'Maybe you should do the same.'

Godfrey snarled at him but said no more. Peter turned to Mrs Stephens.

'You think there'll be a battle at Dunkirk, Miss?'

The teacher shrugged and tried to seem relaxed. She failed dismally.

'I suppose so. There'll have to be a battle of some

sort. But the Royal Navy will be there to back up our troops.'

A battle. People would be killed in a battle, Hannah thought. But she said nothing as the class went back to their seats to learn what they could about the town of Dunkirk.

When it came, the miracle of the little ships humbled them all. Thousands of British soldiers were rescued off the beaches by a tiny fleet of ships, some of them no bigger than rowing boats. Meanwhile, Mr Churchill, the new Prime Minister, skilfully managed to turn defeat into a famous victory.

'We shall defend our island,' he had rumbled in Parliament and on the wireless. 'Whatever the cost may be. We shall fight on the beaches, we shall fight on the landing grounds, in the fields, in the streets and in the hills. We shall never surrender.'

Hannah felt salt tears stinging at her eyes as she listened to Churchill's words and she determined to die bravely, along with all the thousands of others, should the Germans ever arrive here in Mumbles.

'He certainly knows how to make his point,' said her mother.

She was sitting by the kitchen window, reading the paper, while Hannah was getting ready to call on her friends. They had planned to take a bike ride out onto Gower for the day. After all, nobody knew how much longer they would be able to enjoy such pleasures. Since France had fallen, Britain was expected to be the next target. A German invasion was expected at any moment.

'Peter says Mr Churchill is a rabble rouser,' Hannah declared.

Mrs Roberts smiled.

'Really? Well Peter's father supports the Labour Party. Churchill is a Conservative. Mr Longdale would be against him, whatever he said or did. And Peter's just repeating what his father's told him.'

She put down her paper and stared hard at her daughter.

'Don't take everything Peter says as gospel, Hannah. It's an opinion, that's all. Think for yourself, make your own judgements. Maybe we all need a bit of rabble rousing just now. Eh?'

Hannah nodded. She would try. Putting on her coat, she set off to call for Helen. She picked up Peter on the way and shortly the three of them were parking their bikes outside Jack's house.

It was not Jack who answered their knock, however. When the door opened, Mr Davies stood there in his shirtsleeves. There were lines of strain around his eyes and forehead and he looked very old and tired.

'Is Jack ready, Mr Davies?' asked Peter. 'We're going off to Gower for the day.'

The ARP warden stood without speaking and, for a moment, Hannah wondered if he actually recognised any of them. His hands hung loosely by his sides and his shoulders were hunched. Finally, however, he shook his head.

'No, Peter, he's not coming. Not today.'

He turned and started to close the door.

'Are you all right, Mr Davies?' asked Hannah, sensing that something was terribly wrong.

When he turned to face them again, Mr Davies had tears on his cheeks. He was biting his lip in a desperate effort to control his emotions.

'We've just had a telegram from the War Office. Tommy is missing in action. Missing presumed dead.'

The door swung shut and the three friends were left, stunned and speechless, on the doorstep. After a few moments, almost in unison, they turned and went quietly down the street. Not a word was spoken but, almost without realising it, they found themselves wheeling their bikes along the seafront and, soon, they were sitting in Conti's Café.

'Where's your little friend today?' asked Mr Conti. 'He is not with you, eh?'

Peter shook his head and picked up the cups from the counter.

'Not today, Mr Conti,' he said, making his way to the table.

They sat, close to the window, and stared into their cups. Just as Mr Conti had predicted some time ago coffee had become unobtainable. Now they were forced to drink weak, tasteless tea. The tragedy of Jack and his family hung over them like a blanket.

'It's so awful,' whispered Hannah at last. 'I mean, you hear about people being shot or blown up in the war but you never expect it to happen to someone you know.'

Helen shook her head.

'Wait a minute, Hannah, it isn't definite, is it? I mean, Mr Davies only said he was missing. That means they can't find him, doesn't it? He could be captured or wounded or just lost somewhere behind enemy lines. There must have been a lot of confusion at Dunkirk.'

'He might also be dead,' said Peter, firmly. 'You can't avoid that, Helen.'

He paused and drained his tea. Slowly he got to his feet and pulled on his coat. He stared down at the two girls.

'I think I'd better go and tell my sister. She needs to know – before she hears it from somebody by accident.'

Hannah thought back to Tommy and Mary walking together outside this window only a few weeks before. Poor Mary, she thought. She would be devastated.

'All right,' Hannah said. 'Come back afterwards. To tell us how she is. And Peter . . .'

He paused at the door and glanced back towards them. Hannah smiled at him.

'Good luck.'

When Peter had gone Hannah and Helen sat on in the café, staring glumly out of the window. Old Mr Conti seemed to sense that something was wrong and did not disturb them. An air of sadness had seemed to drift down across the day.

'I hate this rotten war,' said Helen, suddenly.

She turned her head and began to cry, silently, into her coat collar.

Chapter Six

Jack was depressed and hurt. He had worshipped his older brother and now, it seemed, Tommy was gone forever. His friends did their best to cheer him up but as the weeks went past and there was no news from France, Jack seemed to retreat more and more into himself.

'I just can't seem to reach him any more,' said Peter one day.

It was late June and the friends were sitting in their favourite spot, the grassy mound overlooking the sea at Langland Bay. The beach was littered with coils of barbed wire and, at the far end of the bay, a soldier in the Local Defence Volunteers stood guard.

The man was old and grey-haired. The LDV was hardly the best defence for the country, Hannah thought, but at least the man on the beach carried a rifle and stared grimly out to sea. What had her mother called the LDV? The Look, Duck and Vanish brigade. She had read in the paper that the LDV was going to be renamed as the Home Guard or some such term. It didn't really concern her. Jack, on the other hand, certainly did.

'You saw Jack,' she said turning towards Peter. 'Did you ask him to come with us today?'

Peter nodded.

'Of course. He just said he wasn't interested. And then he shut the door on me.'

'Well, we can't force him. He'll come out of himself when he's ready. We'll just have to be here when he does.'

They spent the day wandering along the cliff tops. So many parts of the coast had been sealed off and there seemed to be soldiers or LDV men everywhere. Late in the afternoon, the three friends made their way back to Mumbles. Dusk was gathering and the shadows were slowly beginning to lengthen and grow.

As they walked down the hill into town Helen suddenly stopped and pointed down the road.

'Isn't that Jack?'

Hannah squinted through the dusk. A hundred yards further down the hill a small figure was moving slowly along, taking care to keep close to the wall where the shadows thrown by the evening sun were already long and dark.

It was Jack all right, there was no doubt about that. His movements were jerky and he constantly glanced around, as if checking that nobody was following him.

'Where do you think he's going?' asked Helen.

Nobody answered. And then, suddenly, Peter gasped.

'Look!' he said. 'Godfrey Scrivens.'

Jack had come to a halt alongside a dark alleyway. As he stood there, Godfrey Scrivens ghosted out of the opening and came to a halt beside him. The two boys seemed to be in deep conversation. Finally, Godfrey reached out and offered something to the smaller boy. Without a second glance, Jack seized the offering and walked off down the road. Godfrey eased back into the alleyway.

'What was that about?' asked Hannah. 'What did Scrivens give him?'

'It looked like keys,' said Peter, 'but I couldn't swear to it. We're too far away to see properly.'

Without another word the three friends set off down the road. Before they reached the alleyway, however, another figure swept out of the darkness. For a moment, Hannah thought it was Godfrey. Very quickly she realised it was a man, a tall thin man dressed in a pinstripe suit and with a small trilby hat stuck jauntily on his head. He carried a brown suitcase.

'Hello kiddies,' he called, glancing up the road towards them. 'How's tricks, then?'

A spiv, thought Hannah, as she watched the man move quickly off towards the tram stop. Whatever he had in the case was obviously heavy as he had to stop every ten or twenty yards and change hands.

'Who is that?' asked Hannah.

Peter was gazing at the man's back.

'You don't want to know. His name is Truman – my dad calls him Trotty Truman, mainly because he's always on his toes.'

Helen and Hannah stared at him, not understanding.

'On his toes. Always ready to do a runner. He's a crook, a petty thief. And looking at that suitcase I reckon I know what he's up to. The Black Market!'

Rationing had been introduced by the government back in January. Everyone had their ration books and bacon, butter, sugar and meat were all in very short supply. Even sweets were hard to get and there were rumours that they, too, were soon to be added to the ration book.

'The Black Market?' said Helen. 'You mean he's selling things off the ration book?'

Peter nodded. If he was right, Trotty Truman was setting himself up in a new and very lucrative line of business, selling all those goods that people couldn't normally get their hands on. And selling them at high prices, of course.

'The Black Market's illegal, isn't it?'

'It certainly is. Illegal and worth a lot of money for anybody who gets involved. I bet Trotty's making himself a fortune.'

'What sort of things do you think he's selling?' asked Hannah.

'Anything that's hard to get. Items that are rationed. Oh, I don't know, things like butter and bacon. Petrol, too, I suppose. Stolen goods, anyway.'

Hannah frowned. Stolen goods, either from warehouses on the docks or from people's houses and shops . . . Not that Trotty's customers would be worrying much about where they came from.

'Well, well, well! What do we have here?'

At the sound of the familiar weedy voice, the three friends swung around towards the alleyway. Godfrey Scrivens was standing in the shadows, watching them intently. They had forgotten about the boy once

Trotty Truman had taken their attention, so to see him now came as something of a shock.

'What's it to you, Scrivens?' growled Peter, his voice unusually aggressive.

Godfrey held up his hands and grinned. He looked more like a weasel than ever, Hannah thought, trying to be smarmy and friendly like that.

'Only asking,' Godfrey said. 'Trying to be pleasant. Had a nice day, have you?'

Without bothering to wait for an answer, he strolled easily away, laughing to himself. Within a few minutes he was lost in the darkness but the sound of his tuneless whistle echoed back up the hill towards them.

'I wonder what he's up to?' mused Peter. 'Whatever it is, you can bet it'll come to no good.'

Hannah pointed towards the alleyway.

'He was up there with your Trotty Truman,' she said. 'Do you think, maybe, he's helping him with his dealings on the Black Market? Perhaps he's selling things for him. I wouldn't put it past him.'

They all felt the same. Nothing that Godfrey ever said or did would surprise any of them. More worrying than that, however, was the fact that they'd just seen Jack talking to him. Now what exactly did that mean?

'Trotty Truman, eh?' said PC Longdale when they arrived at Peter's house and told his father what they had seen. 'He's been lying low lately – I wondered when he'd surface again.'

He was standing in the garden, in his shirtsleeves.

Like everyone else, the Longdales were starting to grow vegetables. It seemed that there was hardly a free plot of land anywhere in town that didn't have cabbages or potatoes sprouting from the earth. Hannah stared at what had once been Peter's back lawn – now the earth was turned over like a ploughed field.

'Can't you arrest this Trotty Truman?' asked Helen.

The policeman shook his head.

'No, love, I'm afraid not. I'd have to catch him in the act, selling his stolen goods. Or get my hands on the contents of that suitcase you described. Otherwise there's no proof – it's all what we call circumstantial.'

He paused and stared down the garden path to where his wife and daughter were still digging away. It would be pitch dark in a few minutes, Hannah thought, and wondered how much longer they intended to work.

'Black marketing is a rotten trade. It's like taking blood out of our sailors, all the men who are fighting and dying to get the goods here in the first place. They put their lives at risk so that crooks like Trotty Truman can make themselves a fortune. You might as well hold a gun to their heads and shoot them.'

'And the soldiers,' said Peter.

PC Longdale smiled at his son, then glanced back down the path to where Mary was now taking a break, leaning on her spade. She looked sad and strained.

'Yes,' whispered the policeman, 'and the soldiers. Everybody who's fighting to keep us safe. Believe me, if I could I'd lock the little thief away for a long, long time. And if Godfrey Scrivens has got himself involved – well he'll get the same treatment. But until I can catch them . . .'

He left the sentence unfinished and went back to his digging. Peter glanced at Hannah and shrugged.

'There's not much else we can do. I'd better go and help the family dig. Everyone's got to do their bit, haven't they?'

*   *   *

The following day the three friends walked to school and talked things over.

'I really don't care about Godfrey,' said Hannah. 'Or even Trotty Truman, and his Black Market. No, all I care about is Jack. And if he's got himself involved with that pair then all I can say is, God help him.'

All night she had lain and thought about Jack. She couldn't, for the life of her, work out why he was even talking to Godfrey Scrivens, let alone taking things off him.

'Jack wouldn't be so stupid as to get involved with crooks,' said Peter. 'He knows what Godfrey's like. And Trotty? Well you've only got to look at him to see what he's about.'

Hannah shook her head.

'Don't be so sure. Jack's not been himself lately, not since he heard the news about Tommy.'

'Grieving is one thing. Being a crook is something different.'

Hannah knew what Peter was saying but she was not convinced. They went into the school playground, each of them lost in thought. When Mrs Stephens called them for the start of the day they joined the crush of bodies pouring into the hall for assembly. And there they waited.

'What's going on?' asked Helen as she sat, cross-legged on the floor. 'Where's Mr Alexander?'

They only had assembly once a week and Mr Alexander, the headmaster, was always here before everyone else, standing at the front of the hall, defying anyone to speak. His steely gaze was usually more than enough to quell even the most boisterous of temperaments.

Today, however, there was no headmaster and soon the low throb of children's voices, curious and puzzled, began to drum at the air like the engines of enemy bombers. For five minutes they waited.

'Look,' hissed Hannah, suddenly. 'There he is.'

The headmaster, tall and grey-haired, had just come into the hall. As children saw him they began to fall silent, row by row. It was not quick enough for Mr Alexander, however.

'Quiet!' he roared. 'Quiet now!'

He faced the assembled students, eyes keen as a hawk. He seemed to be looking for someone. A terrible feeling of disaster began to gather in Hannah's stomach. She knew that something awful was about to happen.

'Peter Longdale!' barked the headmaster, finally spotting his quarry. 'My office, boy. Now!'

Peter glanced briefly, anxiously, at Hannah, then levered himself to his feet and began to make his way along the row of seated and kneeling children.

'Move quicker, boy,' boomed Mr Alexander, 'if you know what's good for you. The rest of you – not a sound!'

He strode out, not waiting for Peter. There was total silence, now, in the big hall. Hannah felt the fear like a fist in her belly. What on earth had Peter done? She watched his back as he went down the aisle and out of the doorway.

Suddenly she felt a pressure on her leg. Helen was digging an index finger into her thigh.

'Look!' she hissed, pointing towards Godfrey Scrivens.

The school bully was sitting in the same row as them and he was grinning from ear to ear. Hardly able to contain himself, he was laughing and nudging one of his cronies in the row in front. When he saw Hannah and Helen staring, he turned to face them and winked and pointed in their direction.

'One down,' he mouthed. 'Two to go!'

Peter did not come back. They went off to their classrooms and began lessons for the day. Still Peter did not return. By morning break, Hannah could contain herself no longer and, as the other members of her class trooped obediently out to the playground, she approached the teacher's desk.

'Miss? Can I have a word, please?'

Mrs Stephens looked up and shook her head.

'I know what you're going to ask, Hannah. I can't

help you. I can't say anything. And even if I could, it's Peter's business. Peter's and the headmaster's.'

She paused, her eyes sympathetic. Then she put out her hand and gently squeezed Hannah's hand.

'Perhaps you should talk to Mr Alexander.'

Perhaps I should, thought Hannah. She smiled her thanks and strode purposefully out of the door.

'You're not really going to see Mr Alexander?' wailed Helen. 'Hannah, he'll kill you!'

Hannah did not reply. She marched on towards the headmaster's office. Helen stopped at the end of the corridor, unwilling and afraid to come any closer. With eyes wide she watched her friend knock on the head's door.

'Come.'

The voice echoed around the building like an air-raid siren. Gathering her courage, Hannah pushed open the door and went inside.

The room was high and full of light. Mr Alexander sat behind a huge desk in the centre of the room.

'Well?'

Hannah gulped, pushed down her fear and began to speak.

'Please sir, it's about Peter Longdale . . .'

She got no further. With a roar of anger the headmaster smashed his fist onto the desk and leapt to his feet.

'What? You have the temerity to come here and talk to me about that boy – that wretched, awful boy. How dare you?'

Hannah felt tears spring into her eyes but she knew

that she could not stop now. The words poured out in a torrent.

'Please sir, he's my friend, the best friend I've ever had. I don't know what he's done or what trouble he's in, but I've got to help. I want to help him, sir.'

The headmaster glared.

'Help? You can't help. I certainly don't need some nosy little girl poking her . . .'

'I am not being nosy!'

Without realising it, Hannah was shouting. She felt her heart pounding and knew that, whatever it cost her, whatever the consequences, she had to make her point.

'I'm not being nosy. I don't care what he's done. I just want to help him.'

She paused, huge sobs wracking her body.

'Please?'

Mr Alexander glared at her. But, strangely, he did not shout again. Perhaps he recognised the concern and compassion in the girl. Perhaps Hannah's words had taken him by surprise. Whatever it was, he slowly began to soften.

'Sit down, Hannah,' he said, coming from behind his desk and leading her to a chair.

Hannah pulled out her handkerchief and blew her nose. Mr Alexander stood alongside her, awkward and a little embarrassed.

'Better?' he asked.

Hannah nodded.

'Please, Mr Alexander, I only want to help. Whatever he's done, Peter's going to need his friends. He's not bad, sir; he's the most honest and decent person I know. Whatever he's supposed to have done, I know I can help him.'

Mr Alexander bent down alongside her.

'Hannah, I can't tell you what's happened. That wouldn't be fair, wouldn't be right.'

'But how can I help him if I don't know what he's done?'

The headmaster stared at her. He knew this girl was Peter's best friend, that the bond between them was solid and firm. By the end of the day she – like all of the school – would know the story anyway. He frowned and shook his head.

'I really can't tell you, Hannah. But what I can do is give you half an hour – half an hour, mind, that's all – to go and see him. Peter's at home. I've suspended him for the time being. Go and see him. Maybe he'll be glad of your help.'

Hannah nodded. She wiped away the remains of the tears and, before the headmaster could change his mind, shot out of the doorway. Grabbing Helen by the arm, she dragged her along the corridor and out through the school gates. In breathless gasps she explained what was happening.

The two girls tore along the street, coats flying and hair streaming in the breeze. They came to a halt in front of Peter's house, strangely reluctant, now that they were here, to knock on the door. Peter had seen them coming, however, and quickly ushered them inside.

'Should you be here?' he asked as they settled themselves around the table in the kitchen.

Hannah nodded. Peter's face was chalky white. It was clear that he had been frightened, seriously frightened, by what had just gone on.

'Mr Alexander said we could come,' Hannah said. 'So what's it all about?'

Peter tried but failed to force a grin. The girls listened as the story was quickly and easily told.

'They found something in my desk. Ration books. Black Market ration books. There must have been £20 worth, I suppose. Somebody told Mr Alexander they were there. He looked and found them. The rest you know.'

They sat for a few moments without speaking, trying hard to take in the enormity of the problem. Black Market ration books meant stolen ration books. It was a serious crime, one that would mean prison for anybody found guilty. Hannah felt the panic rising in her throat.

'But, you . . . Peter, you . . .'

He smiled at her and shook his head.

'Mr Alexander has suspended me while he's making further enquiries. The trouble is, if the police get involved . . .'

He left the sentence unfinished. With his father being the local policeman, it would mean disgrace for the whole family.

'What did your dad say?' asked Helen.

Peter swallowed. 'He doesn't know yet. Mum's gone to find him.'

They lapsed into silence again. Peter toyed with the fringes of the tablecloth and Hannah tried desperately to find something sensible to say.

'How did those books get there, in your desk?' she asked, eventually.

'Somebody must have planted them. I can't think of any other way, any other reason for them being there. They certainly weren't mine. If they were, I wouldn't have been stupid enough to leave them in my desk. No, somebody planted them there alright.'

'And I think I know who,' said Hannah.

She explained, briefly, about Godfrey Scrivens and what she had seen in assembly after Peter had left. Peter listened.

'It's possible,' he said. 'Maybe that's what he was doing last night when we saw him with Trotty Truman. And . . .'

He stopped, suddenly, not wanting to give words to his thoughts. Hannah nodded.

'Yes. Jack was there as well. You don't think he's involved, do you?'

Peter shrugged. It was something none of them cared to consider, not even to themselves. But the fact remained – they had all seen Jack Davies talking to Godfrey only the night before. And something had exchanged hands between them.

'We've got to get back,' said Hannah suddenly, getting to her feet. 'We'll be back again after school finishes. In the meantime, try not to worry.'

It was a silly comment, she thought, but she had to say something. Peter saw them to the door. They glanced back as they went up the road and he was standing there, on the doorstep, gazing up at the sky. The bright day seemed, suddenly, a lot duller.

Hannah's mind was working feverishly. Not for one second did she think that Peter was guilty. Somebody had set him up and the only person with the motive – the only person with the real hatred to do it – was Godfrey Scrivens.

'I'll sort it out,' she muttered to herself, 'I promise.'

'Pardon?' Helen asked, peering closely into her friend's face.

Hannah smiled. 'I was just making a promise to myself. And to Peter. I was saying that I would sort it out.'

'And how are you going to do that?'

Hannah reached our and took Helen's arm.

'At the moment I don't really know. But I'll find a way. Peter Longdale is as innocent as you and me. And I'm going to prove it. To everyone!'

Chapter Seven

'Is it true?' asked Jack.

It was lunchtime and Hannah and Helen were standing in the playground. Jack had come up, suddenly and unexpectedly, behind them. His face looked old and lined, Hannah decided.

'I'm afraid it is,' she nodded.

She paused and stared hard at Jack.

'Somebody deliberately put those books in Peter's desk. You know he wouldn't have stolen anything like that.'

'I know,' said Jack.

He stood alongside them and said no more. There was a look of infinite sadness on his face and he seemed unsure whether to stay with them or to leave the two girls alone. Hannah reached out and gently laid her hand on his arm.

'Are you all right, Jack? I know it's been hard, what happened with Tommy. But it will get better. Honest it will.'

Jack looked up, his eyes flashing with anger.

'How the hell do you know? You haven't lost a brother.'

The words hurt, knifed into Hannah like a steel blade beneath her ribs. Almost before she knew what she was doing, she had lunged forward and grabbed Jack by the front of his jumper.

'No,' she hissed, 'but I have lost a father.'

Jack winced and threw up his hand, as if to ward off a blow. Instantly the anger in Hannah vanished.

'Where's your watch, Jack?'

The boy glanced down at his wrist, then up into Hannah's eyes. He opened his mouth to speak, to explain, but no words came out. Panic was written across his face.

'Well?'

Hannah pointed towards Jack's forearm.

'Come on. I know what that watch means to you. You haven't taken it off for months. But now it's missing. So where is it?'

She grabbed his arm and held it. The tension was real and tangible. Eventually, however, Jack tore himself away, his hand waving uselessly in the air.

'Lost it,' he mumbled. 'I lost it last week.'

Then he was gone, racing away to the shaded side of the playground. Hannah and Helen stared after him.

'Lost it, my foot,' whispered Hannah. 'Tommy gave him that watch. It meant the whole world to him. And with Tommy dead that was all he had left.'

'So what do you think happened to it?' said Helen.

Hannah's mind was working furiously. Jack certainly wouldn't have lost the watch but he might well have had it taken off him.

'We'll talk to him after school,' she said, 'before we go to Peter's. We need to sort this out today.'

The rest of the school session passed slowly. Hannah found it hard to concentrate on lessons but, eventually, they were dismissed for the day. Four o'clock found them waiting outside the school gates. The playground was deserted, all the pupils having left some time ago, trooping happily away. Of Jack, however, there was no sign.

'Where is he?' Helen muttered. 'It's been twenty minutes since we came out.'

They waited. Another ten minutes went by and then, finally, Jack's slight figure eased furtively out of the main doorway. He glanced nervously around and then came quickly across the playground. It all fitted, thought Hannah: Jack's nervousness, the lost watch – it all made perfect sense. She smiled to herself. Now she just had to prove it.

Jack came swiftly across the tarmac and stopped alongside the gate. Carefully he peered out.

'Looking for someone?' said Hannah.

Jack gasped and leapt a foot into the air. He fell back against the gatepost, breathing heavily through his mouth. Tiny beads of sweat had suddenly broken out across his forehead. Hannah folded her arms and glared at him.

'Or should I say watching out for someone?' she continued.

'Damn you, Hannah!' Jack snarled. 'You nearly made me die of fright.'

Hannah inched towards him and slowly shook her head.

'Not me, Jack, I don't frighten anyone. Godfrey Scrivens, on the other hand, is a bit different.'

'What do you mean? What's Scrivens got to do with it?'

Jack was really scared now. His eyes had grown huge in his head.

'I'll tell you what he's got to do with it,' said Hannah. 'He's the reason you're skulking about here half an hour after school has finished for the day. He's the one that's got you frightened, Jack – so frightened you'll do anything he says.'

She glared directly into his eyes. Her gaze was hard and unwavering. Jack dropped his head, looking anywhere but at the determined and suddenly powerful girl who stood in front of him.

'He took your watch, didn't he? You didn't lose it. Godfrey Scrivens took it off you.'

She pursed her lips and watched him carefully. Jack was shaking his head now, desperately jerking it back and forth in denial, staring pitifully at her and Helen in turn. But his eyes told Hannah that she was right and after a while Jack sensed it. The knowledge broke him. Silently he began to cry.

'Yes, he took it,' he sobbed. 'The other day, he just came up behind me when I was going home from school. His friends grabbed me and held me while he took the watch. I couldn't do anything about it, honestly.'

He lay back against the wall, sobbing and gasping.

'It's all right, Jack,' said Helen. 'Nobody blames you. Godfrey Scrivens is just a big bully. Everybody knows that.'

Hannah shook her head. She had it all now, knew everything there was to know.

'No, Helen, that's not what Jack means. Godfrey

didn't steal the watch for the fun of it. He stole it for a reason, didn't he, Jack?'

The boy wiped a sleeve across his face and tried to sniff back the tears. He glanced at Hannah and smiled, faintly. He seemed almost glad that the truth was finally out.

'He told me I'd get it back if I . . .if I helped him.'

'And you did. What did he ask you for, Jack? The keys to the school?'

Jack nodded. Helen stared, not understanding. All of this was beyond her. She glanced at Hannah, eyes questioning.

'Jack's father is the ARP warden,' Hannah explained. 'He has to have keys to places like the school. After all, a bomb might drop on it or a light might be left on. Then he'd need to get into the building. And get in quickly. So he has a spare set of keys. I've seen them before, lots of times. He keeps them on a hook in the kitchen, doesn't he, Jack?'

Jack said nothing but his silence told Hannah that she was right. Helen, however, was still puzzled.

'But why did Scrivens want the school keys?'

Hannah smiled.

'Do you want to tell her, Jack? No? Because, Helen, he wanted to get into school and plant stolen ration books in Peter's desk.'

A heavy silence fell. Helen stared, first at Hannah and then at Jack. Several times her mouth opened and closed, like a goldfish in a bowl.

'You're wondering how I knew. I didn't, not really, not until just now. Think back, Helen. We saw

Godfrey passing something to Jack only last night. He was giving the keys back. And the ration books? Well, Scrivens is the one with the contact. Trotty Truman, remember? That's who he got them off. Didn't he, Jack?'

The boy stared at her and shrugged.

'I don't know. He just told me he wanted the keys. It was only when I heard about Peter, this morning, that I realised what he'd done.' His face darkened. 'He hates Peter, really hates him. He must do to set him up like that.'

'He hasn't given you the watch back, though, has he, Jack?'

Jack spread his arms in a hopeless gesture of defeat. Tears were close to the surface once more.

'He wouldn't give it back,' Jack said. 'He told me he'd let me have it once he'd got the keys. But he didn't. He just laughed at me.'

'Of course he did,' Hannah smiled. 'He's got you in his power, Jack. As long as he's got that watch you'll do anything he wants. Even set up Peter.'

'I didn't,' Jack protested, 'I didn't. Honest, Hannah, I didn't know what he'd got planned. Not until this morning.'

Hannah glared at him, her eyes unblinking. Maybe Jack really hadn't understood what Godfrey had in mind. But he should have guessed it would involve Peter – and that it was likely to be unpleasant. However she looked at it, she found it impossible to forgive him for what he had done.

'It doesn't matter,' she said, suddenly, coming to a

95

decision. 'All that matters now is that we're going to help Peter out of this jam. And I think I know how we're going to do it.'

*   *   *

The next day dawned wet and windy, almost for the first time that summer. Hannah and Helen were at school early and, soon afterwards, a clearly frightened Jack joined them in the playground. His face was gaunt and grey – Hannah guessed that he had slept very little.

'Morning,' he said, smiling warily at them both.

Hannah ignored him. She was still angry and did not trust herself to speak to him too much.

'Wait here,' she muttered, shortly. 'I won't be long.'

Helen and Jack stared at her. There was a hardness and determination about the girl that they had not seen before. So they stood and waited while Hannah slipped into the school building. Jack said nothing but moved silently and miserably into the shelter of the wall. Absent-mindedly he began to pick at an exposed piece of mortar.

Ten minutes later, Hannah was back. The rain had increased and both Helen and Jack felt clammy and wet. Yet nothing on God's earth would have made either of them move before Hannah gave permission.

'Right,' she declared, approaching them as they waited in the lee of the wall. 'It's all set. Come on, Helen, let's get in out of the rain. Jack, you know what you've got to do. Just make sure he arrives before school starts. Clear?'

Jack nodded, glumly.

'Are you sure about this, Hannah? What if it doesn't work? He's not stupid, you know.'

Hannah glared at him and slowly shook her head. The last thing she needed just now was an in-depth discussion with Jack.

'We've talked about this till I'm blue in the face. I'm not going to start again. You go and get him now.'

With Helen trailing in her wake, Hannah turned and went into the school building. They sat at their desks and waited. Neither of them spoke but their minds were working furiously. Hannah hated to admit it, but her scheme was risky, decidedly risky. What if Godfrey refused to come? What if . . .? She shook her head and tried hard to think of something different.

The minutes seemed to drag past. In spite of her determination, Hannah felt the tension in her limbs. Relax, she whispered, everything is fine. It's all going according to plan.

Suddenly, there came a grumble of voices from the corridor outside. Helen glanced nervously across the aisle. Hannah raised her hand in acknowledgement. They were coming.

'What does she want to see me about?'

Godfrey's voice was unmistakable. He was obviously standing just outside the classroom. A low mumble, impossible to make out, responded. That was Jack, trying to answer the question, yet not give the game away.

The classroom door swung suddenly open, smashing back against the partition wall. The noise echoed like an explosion around the school. Despite herself, Hannah jumped.

'Well?'

Godfrey Scrivens stood in the doorway. His lanky body seemed to fill the frame. Behind him, Hannah could see the smaller figure of Jack, lurking quietly in the corridor.

'I want to talk to you,' said Hannah, trying hard to keep her voice clear and strong. 'About Peter.'

'What about him?'

Godfrey was flippant, his voice cocky and arrogant. Yet despite his tone, the boy was clearly intrigued. He moved into the classroom, swaggering across the floor, and came to a halt in front of Hannah's desk. She suddenly realised just how tall Godfrey really was – no wonder Jack was scared of him.

'I want to know why you set him up.'

Godfrey laughed. The sound was low and menacing – humour was the last thing it brought to mind. Menacingly, the bully pointed his finger at Hannah.

'Listen, girl, I didn't set him up. It's not my fault if he's a thief – and not even a good thief! He's a thief who gets himself caught by old man Alexander.'

Hannah steadily held his gaze. Slowly, carefully, serenely, she smiled at him.

'Oh, but he's not a thief, Godfrey. As you know very well. You see, secrets have a habit of getting out. I know you put those ration books in his desk. And, more importantly, I know how you did it. Would you like me to tell you? I can do that, can't I, Jack?'

Godfrey glanced urgently, briefly, towards Jack. The smaller boy was still standing at the doorway but he was looking firmly at the ground. Godfrey turned back to face Hannah.

'What the hell do you mean?'

'I know you got the school keys from Jack – the spare set that his father keeps for emergencies. You took Jack's watch so that he'd do whatever you asked – like getting you the keys. And then you came here and put those books in Peter's desk.'

Godfrey sniggered.

'You don't know what you're talking about,' he blustered. 'You're just making things up to try and help your friend.'

'Am I?' said Hannah.

She watched him, standing in front of her, so arrogant and full of himself. He really did think that he was safe.

'I saw you the other night,' Hannah said. 'I saw you with Trotty Truman. And I saw you giving the keys back to Jack. I saw you, Godfrey.'

The bully blanched, suddenly scared. There was something about this that he didn't like. Things were getting out of control.

'You just prove it,' he shouted. 'You saw me? Well it's your word against mine. You can't prove a thing.'

'Oh, but I can,' said Hannah. 'You see I've been speaking to Trotty Truman. Not just me. PC Longdale was there as well. And Trotty told him everything. He told us that he gave you the books and why.'

Hannah knew she had Godfrey on the back foot. The boy was rattled – it was time to hit him again.

'Twenty pounds worth of ration books? That was nothing to him, not with the money he's been making. Just an investment, really. The way he looked at it, once he'd given you the books he'd have you eating out of his hands. You'd be running about, doing all his errands, maybe even selling some of his Black Market goods for him. After all, nobody would suspect a schoolboy, would they?'

She paused and lay back in her chair.

'You know, Godfrey, he'd have really cleaned up. Peter would have been sent away to Reformatory School and the whole family would be in disgrace. The police would have been forced to send PC Longdale away. Well, he couldn't be allowed to stay here. Oh, Trotty would have been king of the whole jungle. He'd have made a real killing.'

Godfrey's mouth dropped open and he staggered back against the desk behind him.

'They're going to send Peter away? To a Reformatory?'

Hannah glared at him.

'Stealing ration books? Dealing in the Black Market? They're criminal offences. Still, now that Trotty's told the truth it'll probably be you who gets sent away. Not Peter.'

Godfrey's face had gone chalky white. His eyes bulged like marbles and his breath came in short shallow gasps.

'You've really seen Trotty? He's coughed?'

Hannah nodded. The lie came easily but it was good to see Godfrey frightened at last. He had shown no remorse, no mercy, not for Peter and not for Jack either. Maybe Jack was the one she felt most sorry for after all. Godfrey had taken advantage of him, knowing how low he was after the death of his brother Tommy, and used him to achieve his own ends. So now Hannah smiled up at Godfrey and shrugged.

'Oh, Trotty's coughed all right. The police will be here in an hour. I should think they'd like to talk to you.'

Godfrey gulped. It was as if somebody had punched him, hard, in the stomach. He staggered across the aisle and sat down heavily behind the nearest desk.

'You've got to help me, Hannah. I only did it to get back at Peter. After that time with the 'vacees. After he showed me up like that.'

He stopped and glared at Helen. Clearly the old hatred hadn't yet died.

'Okay, so I put the damned books in his desk. It served him right for what he did. But I never thought they'd send him away. I just thought he'd get into trouble with Mr Alexander, maybe get the cane or be suspended for a while. Honest.'

A sudden heavy footfall made Godfrey spin around. With a sharp intake of breath he saw Mr

Alexander and Mrs Stephens coming down the aisle towards him. He stumbled to his feet, face red and eyes wide with horror.

'Mr Alexander, sir, we're just talking. Only talking sir, we . . .'

The headmaster came to a halt in front of the boy and Godfrey's voice trailed off. Mr Alexander glared at him and slowly pointed his finger.

'Don't bluster, Godfrey. We heard everything, Mrs Stephens and I, from behind that screen at the front of the class – we've been there the whole time.'

He gestured to where Mrs Stephen's screen stood alongside the teacher's desk. Her map of Europe, with its little red pins and pieces of coloured cotton, was still stuck onto it.

Godfrey tried to speak. His mouth opened, then closed. Nothing came out. Finally defeated, he fell back heavily in the chair and tears began to course down his cheeks.

'I'm sorry,' he cried. 'Sorry. Please don't tell the police, sir. Please?'

The headmaster frowned.

'We'll see how sorry you are in a few moments,' he said. 'My office, now.'

Together they went out. By now Helen was bouncing up and down in her seat, unable to contain her excitement any longer.

'You've done it, Hannah!' she shouted. 'You've done it!'

Hannah felt drained and empty. She sat behind her desk, eyes fixed on the floor ahead of her. It worked, she kept saying to herself. The bluff worked. Suddenly, she felt a hand on her arm and looked up into the kindly features of Mrs Stephens.

'Well done, Hannah. I'm glad you persuaded Mr Alexander and me to take part in your little trick. That screen certainly made a great hiding place. The truth is out and it's all down to you.'

Hannah shook her head and gazed, pleading, into the teacher's eyes.

'I don't care about that, Miss. I care about Peter. Can he come back to school now?'

Mrs Stephens nodded.

'I suggest you go and tell him what's happened. Then get him back here – it's history first period. And you know that's his favourite subject.'

Hannah was halfway through the door when Jack spoke. His voice was low and wary.

'Hannah? Do you think I can come too? I've probably got some apologising to do.'

Hannah's first inclination was to walk on and ignore him. Jack had got them into this whole mess in the first place. Then she glanced up and saw Helen's beaming face. Suddenly, she remembered what it was like for someone – anyone – to be without friends.

'He's learned his lesson,' Helen whispered, 'don't you think, Hannah?'

Hannah stared at her, then swung around to face Jack. Hostility clung to her words.

'I don't know if I can ever forgive you, Jack.'

The boy lowered his head, misery clouding around

him like a mist. Then Hannah reached out and put her hand on his arm.

'But Peter probably will,' she smiled. 'Come on. Let's go and tell him the good news.'

Chapter Eight

It was a tense summer. With most of Europe under German control, the whole country sat watching, waiting for the expected invasion. Prime Minister Churchill had summed up the mood perfectly.

'Hitler knows he will have to break us in these islands,' he had declared, 'or lose the war.'

And Churchill, like everybody else in Britain, had no intention of being broken. But they all believed that it was only a matter of time before the invasion barges came storming across the English Channel. Then would come the fight, a fight like no-one had ever seen before. They were ready for it. Some were almost looking forward to it

'I wish we were in Kent or somewhere like that,' declared Jack.

They were sitting on the tarmac of the school playground. Jack was poking idly with a lollypop stick at a bubble of tar that the hot day had brought up on the yard. He spoke quietly but seriously. Since his brother had gone missing an air of sadness had surrounded him. Peter had soon forgiven him for the business with Godfrey Scrivens but there remained a certain tension in the air. He had been accepted back into the group but things were not the same. Jack's behaviour, his involvement with Godfrey, had changed things.

'What was that, Jack?' asked Hannah. 'What did you say?'

'I just said I wished we were living in Kent. Then we could see some of the air battles, the dog fights between the Spitfires and the German Meschersmitts.'

Hannah shook her head. She could understand Jack wanting revenge on the people who had killed his brother but didn't he realise that people were dying up there in the skies? Every day there were battles and air attacks on aerodromes and radar stations in the south east of England. It was all too far away for Jack, however,

'Down here,' he complained, 'we get to see nothing. No planes, no German bombers. Maybe the odd Spitfire flies over but that's all. It's so boring.'

'I don't want to see any German bombers,' Helen offered. 'My mum and dad wrote last week and said that there's not enough air-raid shelters for all the people in London.'

Jack snorted. 'They've got their Anderson Shelters in the garden, haven't they?'

By now most of the houses in Britain had their own air-raid shelters, makeshift contraptions out in the gardens or Morrison Shelters for indoors, things that looked like huge steel tables. They had been provided free of charge in the early months of the war.

'Mum and Dad don't have a garden,' said Helen. 'We live in a flat. So all they've got is the public shelter at the end of the road – as long as there's room. Or they use the Morrison Shelter in the living room. I don't know how strong that is. And you wouldn't fancy spending the night stuck under your kitchen table, would you?'

Jack frowned and said no more. Peter reached over and took Helen's arm.

'It's probably safer in the public shelter,' he said. 'No house could ever stand a direct hit. They're better off in the public shelter.'

'Time for lessons,' announced Hannah, catching sight of Mrs Stephens coming out onto the top step and waving them all inside.

They climbed to their feet and headed off across the playground. As they did so, Godfrey Scrivens suddenly appeared from around the corner and came racing past them. He cannoned into Jack, sending the small boy sprawling into the tarmac.

'Hey, watch it!' called Peter, helping Jack to his feet.

Godfrey had stopped alongside them. He sneered at Peter but, Hannah noticed, he kept his distance. It had been like that ever since Peter had returned to school. Godfrey was clearly wary of him – and of Hannah, too. Jack and Helen, on the other hand, seemed to come in for more than the usual share of bullying.

'Next time, get out of my way,' Godfrey sneered.

He stuck out his chin and clenched his fist. Jack flinched. Godfrey laughed and disappeared into the school building.

'That awful boy,' said Helen. 'I don't know why Mr Alexander lets him come here after what he did to you, Peter.'

Peter smiled, took off his glasses and carefully wiped them with his shirtsleeve.

'What did you expect? He gave evidence against

Trotty Truman, evidence that helped him get convicted and sent down. So the magistrate was bound to look leniently on him. And school? Well, he had his week's suspension. He was never going to get more. His dad is a local councillor, you know.'

'He certainly hasn't learned his lesson, that's for sure,' said Hannah. 'He's more of a bully now than ever.'

They went into the coolness of the main building, walking slowly to get their eyes accustomed to the light. It may have been darker inside the building but the heat was oppressive, stifling and heavy. None of them relished the idea of an afternoon studying maths and geography.

'Shall we go to Conti's after school?' asked Hannah. 'I think by then we'll all be ready for something cold to drink.'

The others nodded and they went into the classroom. Mrs Stephens's map on the front screen was now full of pins and coloured ribbons. With battles being fought so close to home, however, Mrs Stephens and most of the class had lost their enthusiasm for following the course of the war.

Once school had finished for the day, the four friends quickly gathered together their belongings and headed off down the hill to the sea front. It was still very warm, the sky bright blue and cloudless.

'Thank goodness that's over,' sighed Helen. 'I swear I actually fell asleep during the last lesson.'

Hannah agreed. Her own eyes had closed more than once during the long afternoon.

As they went down the hill there was a roar of aircraft engines and three single-wing fighters swept suddenly overhead. They banked to the right and disappeared from view beyond the hill to the west of the bay.

'Spitfires,' Jack announced. 'Out on patrol from Pembrey aerodrome. Not that three fighters are going to find much down here. They'd be better employed packing up and heading for Kent or Sussex. That's where all the action is.'

Peter stared at him.

'Maybe that's why they're here. If the Air Ministry moved them you can bet your bottom dollar the Germans would attack Swansea or Cardiff next day. They're being held in reserve, Jack, as a deterrent.'

Jack did not reply, but Hannah could see that he was thinking about Peter's words.

They were twenty or thirty yards short of the café when Peter pulled up sharply. He pointed down the road.

'What on earth's going on?' he frowned.

A large crowd had gathered on the pavement outside Conti's Café. An army truck was parked against the kerb and two soldiers, rifles held ready in their hands, were leaning against the bonnet. Hannah glanced at Peter and, almost in unison, they hurried forward.

'My father's here,' said Peter. 'I wonder what he's doing?'

PC Longdale was standing outside the café door, keeping the crowd back from the entrance and urging everyone to stay calm and still. Elbowing and pushing, the four friends made their way to the front. The policeman saw them and promptly shook his head. Sighing, he held up his hand.

'You can't come in here,' he said, staring at Peter. 'Not today. Best you go home, all of you.'

The crowd behind them was restless and noisy. Several of them, Hannah noticed, were locals, young men who had not yet been called up for the army. Most of the group, however, she had never seen before. They looked rough and she guessed they had come from Swansea – probably after several hours in one of the pubs in Mumbles. And the mood soon turned nasty.

'Bloody Eyeties!' called a voice from somewhere in the mass of people.

'String 'em up!' shouted somebody else.

A stone came flying out of the crowd. There was a bang and the huge plate glass window at the front of the café shattered into a million pieces. Like crystal raindrops the glass fell to the pavement. A loud cheer and a burst of laughter rose from the assembled spectators.

'That'll teach the bloody foreigners,' laughed a man at the front of the group.

PC Longdale strode forward and stood nose to nose with him.

'Open your mouth once more,' he snarled, 'and you'll be spending the next week inside.'

The man dropped his head and said nothing. PC Longdale turned to the crowd and raised his arms.

'All right, that's enough. Any more damage and I'll arrest the lot of you for breach of the peace. And if you don't think I can do it, I've got a couple of soldiers here who'd just love to help me out.'

He pointed towards the army truck. The soldiers inched forward and carefully lifted their rifles.

'I'm serious,' called PC Longdale. 'There's no call to damage property – whoever it belongs to.'

The crowd rumbled its discontent but nobody threw any more stones. For a few moments PC Longdale glared at them.

'Right,' he called, at last. 'I want you all to disperse now. Just clear off home and we'll say no more about this.' He pointed at the smashed window. 'Go on!' he shouted. 'Go now!'

For a few minutes nobody moved. Then, slowly, one by one, people began to slip away. One or two malcontents hung around, obviously reluctant to leave. A few quiet words from the policeman, however, and even they soon drifted off down the road towards the nearest bar or somewhere they could find something to drink.

Soon, only the four friends were left standing outside the café. The glass from the broken window lay like a silent accusation on the pavement. Hannah shook her head, disbelief and lack of understanding mirrored in her eyes.

'What's been going on?' she whispered. 'What's it all about?'

PC Longdale turned towards them and pointed down the road.

'You lot, too,' he said. 'There's nothing for you to see here. Get off home.'

Before they could move or question, there was a sudden flurry from inside the café and Mr Conti came out. He was accompanied by two tall men dressed in suits and trilby hats. It didn't take the greatest imagination in the world to work out that they were plainclothes policemen.

'My window!' wailed the café owner. 'What happened to my window?'

The two plainclothes men glared at PC Longdale, their eyes questioning and accusing at the same time.

'There was a little trouble with the crowd,' the policeman explained. 'It's over now.'

'But who will pay for this?' called Mr Conti. 'Why did they do it, why?'

One of the plainclothes men took him by the arm and led him towards the waiting truck.

'We'll get it repaired, sir,' he said. 'Or boarded up. PC Longdale will see to that. But at the moment I think you have rather more to worry about than a bit of broken glass.'

At that moment, Mr Conti caught sight of the four friends.

'Peter!' he called. 'Hannah!'

He wrenched himself free and started to run towards them. The policemen grabbed him by the arm and twisted it viciously behind his back. Mr Conti cried out in pain.

'Leave him alone,' Hannah shouted. 'You're hurting him.'

112

She leapt across the pavement before PC Longdale could stop her. Urgently, she clutched at Mr Conti's hand. The plainclothes policeman was flustered and stepped back in alarm. Mr Conti caught Hannah to him and pulled her tight. As he did so he glanced towards the upstairs window, to the flat where he had lived for thirty years with his wife. Old Mrs Conti stood, like a ghost, sobbing at the window. Her face was twisted in pain, contorted by the tears.

'Hannah!' cried Mr Conti. 'They're arresting me. Me? I have never committed a crime in my life but they're arresting me.'

The second plainclothes policeman came quickly over the pavement and pushed himself between Hannah and the café owner. He glared at the girl and spoke sharply to Mr Conti.

'We're not arresting anyone, sir, just taking you away for internment. It's the law, Mr Conti. All enemy aliens are to be interned for the duration of the war. Italy declared war on us, you know. We didn't ask for trouble from Mussolini. You want to blame somebody you go and blame your blessed Mussolini.'

Mr Conti was confused and uncertain. He dithered on the edge of the pavement.

'He's not my Mussolini. And what is an enemy alien? I am not alien. I have lived here for thirty years. This is my home, not Italy.'

Before he could say any more, the policemen each seized an arm and bundled him into the back of the truck. Mr Conti collapsed onto one of the seats and sat, slumped, like a limp rag doll. The soldiers and policemen climbed in behind him. One of them banged on the roof of the cab and the lorry shot away down the road towards Swansea.

Hannah turned to face her friends and PC Longdale.

'What was all that about? What happened?'

The policeman stared at her and did not reply. Helen put her arm around her friend's shoulder and hugged her.

'Don't worry, Hannah. It'll be alright.'

Hannah shook her head, tears pricking at her eyes. How could everything be alright? What had happened here today was inhuman, she thought. You might have expected it in Hitler's Germany, but surely not here in Britain?

'I'm sorry about this,' said PC Longdale, 'but there's nothing I can do. As the Inspector said, the government has decided to intern all Italian and German aliens, people like Mr Conti. Things like this have been happening today all over the country.'

He paused and stared across the road to where the sea rippled gently along the beach. It seemed so quiet and peaceful after what had just gone on. Hannah knew that she would remember this moment – the sight of Mr Conti, glum and broken in the back of the lorry – for the rest of her life. Whatever PC Longdale said, nothing could ever put it right.

The policeman turned towards the four friends. For some reason he was unable to look directly at his son and spoke with his eyes on the broken window.

'Mr Conti will be locked away in an internment camp with lots of other Italian nationals. He'll probably be there for as long as the war lasts. Don't worry about him, he'll be well looked after – we're not Nazis, after all!'

He frowned and nodded towards the mound of broken glass.

'I think he'll be better off in a camp. You saw how the crowd was behaving here today. There's an awful lot of anti-Italian feeling around at the moment. I'm not sure we could keep him safe if he was allowed to stay here.'

Hannah stared up at the flat above the café. She could hear the sound of distant sobbing but Mrs Conti had fallen back from the window and could no longer be seen. PC Longdale followed Hannah's gaze.

'She'll be fine, Hannah, once she gets over the shock. Her daughter-in-law is coming for her tonight. Her husband, the Contis' son, has been interned too. So all the women of the family will stay together for a while.'

'But where will they go?' asked Helen. 'Where will they stay?'

The policeman shrugged.

'As far as I know they're going to be staying at the son's place in the Rhondda Valley – Porth, I think. They'll have to register as resident aliens up there.'

He paused and drew himself up to his full height.

'I'm afraid it means the end of the café – at least for a while. Anyway, it's not my problem. I've got to get this window sorted. I suggest you lot head on home. There's nothing more to see here.'

They went along the seafront, hearts heavy and full of sadness.

'Poor Mr Conti,' said Helen, 'being dragged away from his family like that. It's too awful to think about.'

Hannah glanced across at her. It was obvious what she was thinking about – the distress of the Italian family had brought home her own sense of loneliness and isolation.

'It's not as if he's a threat to national security, is it?' said Peter suddenly. 'I mean he must be sixty, at least. What did they think he was going to do? Signal to Italian submarines out in the Channel? Or bring in paratroopers to his back garden?'

Jack stared at him, his face set in a determined frown. He stood with his hands on his hips.

'Hang on a minute,' he said. 'He is an Italian. And they are the enemy – just like the Germans. I wouldn't trust any of them.'

Hardly able to believe what she had heard, Hannah swung around to confront him. Anger burned in her belly and her eyes blazed.

'Shut up, Jack!' she stormed. 'Just shut up! Sometimes, oh, sometimes you're just too stupid for words.'

She tore off down the road, leaving the others staring after her. Jack spread his hands, genuinely confused.

'What did I say?'

Helen stared at him. Despairingly, she shook her head.

'One day,' she whispered, 'one day, Jack, you might just learn.'

She turned and followed her friend up the road.

Chapter Nine

With the going of Mr Conti, things began to change. Despite the continued fine weather the days seemed darker, more ominous, and the threat from Germany grew steadily.

In the skies over Britain, the battle raged. The papers were full of stories about 'the few', as the pilots has been christened. Then, in July, came the first of Swansea's casualties.

'What's that noise?' asked Hannah's mother one night.

They were sitting in the lounge, listening to the wireless. Big-hearted Arthur Askey was telling his silly jokes and singing pointless songs. Hannah didn't like him – Bigheaded Arthur Askey she called him. So she was glad at her mother's interruption and looked up eagerly.

A high-pitched whine seemed to be coming from outside. Hannah's eyes widened.

'That's the air-raid siren,' she said. 'It's an air raid, Mum. We're having an air raid. Come on, we need to get into the shelter.'

They turned out the light and went into the back garden. Out here the noise was much louder, reverberating off the walls, the houses and the surrounding hills. To the east, towards Swansea, searchlights probed the night sky, reflecting off the low cloud base and the string of fat barrage balloons that swung on their moorings above the town. From somewhere overhead came the insistent drumming of aircraft engines.

'German bombers,' said Mrs Roberts. 'You can't mistake those engines. Heading for the docks, I reckon.'

They went into the Anderson shelter and sat side by side on one of the bunks. The shelter was cramped and dark, smelling of damp earth, but it felt safe in there. From outside came the whine of falling bombs, quickly followed by the crump of far-off explosions. The shelter shook.

Hannah held her mother's hand and grimaced with each bang. The raid was a long way off, however, and finally she dropped off to sleep, her head resting easily on her mother's shoulder.

'Hannah!'

Her mother was gently shaking her, easing her back into wakefulness. Hannah yawned and sat up. She felt stiff and tired.

'The All-Clear's just sounded. Let's go in and get to bed.'

A deep red glow lit the eastern sky as they climbed out of the shelter and went along the garden path. There was a faint smell of sulphur in the air.

'Looks like they've hit something,' said Mrs Roberts. 'Something quite big, I'd say.'

The roar of a nearby anti-aircraft gun suddenly echoed through the night. There was a flash of light, then darkness again.

'Typical,' sighed Mrs Roberts. 'They manage to

open fire when the bombers have been and gone. God knows how we're ever going to win this war!'

Hannah had heard that there were only three anti-aircraft guns for the whole of Swansea. She didn't know for sure but she supposed it was quite possible. So far, the town hadn't been much of a target for enemy bombers – until tonight.

It wasn't the first time Swansea had been attacked but this was certainly the worst bombing it had suffered so far. When Hannah and Helen walked to school next day everybody was talking about the raid. Jack was nearly beside himself with excitement.

'Twelve men got killed,' he said, almost gleefully. 'Dockers, they were.'

'You don't need to be quite so pleased about it,' Helen snapped. 'Twelve dead men means twelve families without a father. Or . . . .'

She stopped, realising what she had been about to say. 'Without a brother' would have been too cruel. When they reached the school playground the first thing they saw was a crowd of children gathered against the far wall. In the centre of the crowd stood Godfrey Scrivens.

'Shrapnel,' he was declaring, proudly displaying a lump of what looked like molten iron. 'My dad got it off the docks last night.'

Hannah frowned. The shrapnel was hard and evil. She thought, bitterly, about thousands of similar objects cutting through the night sky, ripping into buildings and people. She turned away, only to run head first into Jack.

'Did you see what Godfrey's got?' he asked, breathlessly. 'I'm going to ask my dad to find me some.'

Then he was gone, to take another look at Godfrey's treasure.

As summer wore on, the Battle of Britain continued unabated. August came and with it the summer holidays. It was so different from the summer of last year, Hannah decided. Then, despite the looming threat of Nazi Germany, the world had seemed so much calmer, so much more innocent. Now war had come in earnest, fear and hatred seemed to be everywhere.

The four friends tried to enjoy their summer holiday but it was hard with so much going on only a hundred or so miles away. There were a few bombing raids on Swansea and other south Wales towns but, for the most part, it was a question of following the conflict in the newspapers and on the wireless.

They were all glad when September finally arrived and it was time to return to school. A new anti-aircraft battery was posted to the area, setting up their guns on Mumbles Hill behind the town. More soldiers and artillery took up positions on the seafront and on the road to Swansea. The number of barrage balloons floating like giant pears above the town seemed to have doubled in number in just a few days.

'Do you think somebody knows something we don't?' asked Peter, staring across the bay. 'It certainly looks like we're building up for something big.'

In the second week of September came the news of heavy daylight raids on London and Peter's question seemed to have been answered. Hundreds had been killed, the papers said, and Helen was almost distraught with worry.

'They're the worst raids so far,' she told her friends. 'It seems like Hitler's changed his tactics.'

Peter nodded, sagely. 'You're right. Up till now he's been trying to knock out the airfields so the RAF can't fly. Now it seems he's decided to try for the city instead.'

'Can't beat the RAF,' Jack gloated. 'That's why he's increased the raids. Now we'll see some action, I bet.'

Helen stared at him, her mouth working and a nervous tick beating in her cheek. Sometimes, Jack could be so insensitive, Hannah told herself. Anybody could see that Helen was frightened, not for herself but for her mother and father back in London.

'They'll be all right,' she reassured Helen, putting her arm around her friend's shoulder. 'Try not to think about it.'

She turned towards Jack.

'And do me a favour, Jack? Just think a little bit before you start to speak in future.'

It was like asking the boy not to gloat about his cigarette card collection. As the days went by, however, Helen's anxiety only increased. No matter how often she received letters from home she could not push down the fear that constantly rose like bile in her throat.

The German bombers came back to London time after time, raiding by day and by night. Soon it seemed as if the whole city was a mass of flame and rubble. Through it all, Helen sat and worried, cried herself to sleep at night and prayed that everything would be all right. With her friends, she was quiet and reserved but it was clear to all of them that her mind was working furiously.

So it was no surprise when Hannah called for her one Saturday in early October to find Helen with her coat already on and a small brown suitcase in her hand.

'What's going on?' Hannah asked with a sinking sensation in her stomach. 'What are you doing?'

Helen smiled, shyly, but with determination. Hannah hadn't seen her friend smile for several weeks. She knew she should be pleased to see that grin now but the coat and case were acting like a cold flannel on her senses.

'I'm going home,' Helen said. 'Today.'

Hannah glanced urgently around but there was no sign of Mrs Livingstone. Helen reached out and squeezed her friend's arm.

'My aunt's not here. She doesn't know I'm going. I've left her a letter, telling her everything. It's better that way – I really couldn't face telling her in person.'

She paused, her eyes suddenly desperate and pleading. After a moment she turned away, gazing out of the kitchen window.

'Please, Hannah,' she said, 'don't try to stop me,

don't try to persuade me to stay. I'm so frightened about going back. The thought of all those bombs, people being killed – well, it terrifies me. I don't want to see places I know, places I love, blitzed and bombed, burned to the ground.'

'So why go?' said Hannah, crossing the room to stand alongside her. 'If that's how you feel, stay here. Don't go.'

Helen shook her head.

'I've got to. I may be frightened to go back but I'm even more frightened to stay. I need to know that my mum and dad are safe. I need to be with them. You can see that, can't you? Please Hannah, don't ask me to stay. It wouldn't take much. I'm not very strong – I need you on my side, not against me.'

Despite what she said, there was something in her voice, something very powerful and strong about her, something Hannah had never seen before. She knew that she should argue, should try and convince Helen to stay here in safety, but she also knew that she would say nothing. Helen had to do what was right for her. And so, reluctantly, she nodded.

'I'll come to the station with you,' she said.

They went down the road to the tram stop. Soon they were rattling along the seafront towards Swansea. Over culverts, embankments and bridges they clattered. Helen did not speak but, after a while, she reached out for Hannah's hand and held it tightly.

The station in Swansea was crowded with people, most of them soldiers and airmen with huge canvas bags on their shoulders. Nobody noticed the two girls. Helen bought her ticket and a platform ticket for Hannah.

'It's a good job I've been saving my pocket money,' she grinned happily. 'Otherwise I'd never have afforded the fare. Look, I've even packed some sandwiches for lunch. It's going to be a long journey and I'll probably have to walk from Paddington. But it's exciting, isn't it?'

Her eyes shone, full of hope and expectation. Hannah shook her head, trying to dispel a sudden feeling of doom and disaster. She knew, surely and certainly, that Helen was heading into danger.

'Please stay, Helen,' she said. 'I'm frightened for you.'

She was standing on the platform alongside the carriage, clouds of steam and smoke rolling down the track. Helen had already boarded the train and was leaning out of the carriage window, beaming happily. Behind her the compartment was full of soldiers. Hannah glanced at them, unsure and afraid.

'Don't worry, missy,' laughed one of the soldiers. 'We'll look after her.' He turned to his companions. 'Got a kid that age myself,' he said.

He had a cockney accent and when he smiled Hannah could see big gaps in his teeth,

'Make sure you do,' Hannah said, glaring at him.

The soldiers laughed and the cockney saluted. Hannah glanced urgently at Helen.

'Please stay here,' she said.

Helen shook her head, suddenly sad.

'You know I can't do that. But I'll write. I promise

– every week if you like. I'll miss you, Hannah, more than you'll know, but I have to do this. I can't stay here any longer, not without Mum and Dad. It's all right for you, you belong here, I don't. I belong in London.'

The loud blast of the guard's whistle echoed down the platform and with a sudden jolt the train began to move. Gradually it picked up speed. Hannah started to walk, keeping pace with the carriage and her friend but knowing, already, that it was too late.

'Take care, Helen,' she cried. 'Be careful.'

She reached out for her friend's hand. Their fingers touched once, briefly, then Hannah was left stranded as the train pulled away. Helen waved from the open window, then she was lost in a cloud of white smoke. When it had cleared, Helen and the train had gone.

*   *   *

Helen was as good as her word. She wrote regularly, letters arriving for Hannah almost every week. They were full of news about her school, her parents and what she did with her friends at the weekends. The only thing she never mentioned was the bombing. Hannah knew, however, that it must be bad, that every night the Heinkels and Dorniers would come droning over the city, turning factories and houses into a mass of flames and rubble.

'Heard from Helen this week?' asked Peter as they walked to school one morning.

It was early December and the weather was icy

cold. Christmas was only a few weeks away but, this year, there were so many shortages – food, clothes, luxury goods of any kind – that it was hard to get excited about it.

It had already been announced that, after Christmas, there would be no more bananas, that no more fresh or tinned fruit would be imported. The space in the ships, Churchill insisted, was needed for the war effort. So Christmas? Let it come, let it do its worst.

Hannah smiled at Peter's question and passed across Helen's latest letter.

'Got it yesterday,' she said. 'According to Helen, nearly all the evacuees who went away in the first days of the war have gone back. It's true, isn't it? She's gone and even Ellie and Cathy – remember the two little girls, friends of Helen's? – even they've slipped away, back to London.'

Peter shrugged, turning the letter over in his hand.

'It can't be helped, I suppose. I know I'd rather be with my family if there was danger – rather than being stuck here, miles away, not knowing what's going on back home.'

He handed the letter back and frowned. He gazed around, puzzled and unsure.

'I wonder where Jack's got to this morning?'

It was certainly unusual, Hannah thought. Jack was normally out at his gate, waiting for them every morning. Today he had not been there at the end of his path and, after waiting for a few minutes, they had walked on to school without him.

'He's probably out collecting shrapnel,' laughed Peter. 'Did you know that's his latest craze? He's got dozens of different bits. And shell cases. They're all over his bedroom. He showed me a piece the other night – it was still red hot.'

Hannah smiled. Jack would never change. They went into the school playground and, soon, Mrs Stephens called them in for lessons. Strangely, there was still no sign of Jack and when the teacher called his name on the register she was greeted only by silence.

'Hannah? Peter?' asked Mrs Stephens. 'Do you know where Jack is today?'

They shook their heads and at that moment they heard the sound of feet racing down the corridor. The door crashed open, smashing back against the partition with a resounding boom. Everyone jumped. Jack stood, panting, in the doorway.

'He's alive!' he yelled. 'He's alive!'

Mrs Stephens moved quickly to the door and took Jack by the arm. Gently, she led the boy to his seat.

'Now then,' she said. 'Tell us all about it.

Jack sat back, breathlessly, in the chair. His face was beaming and he gazed urgently around, trying to pick out his friends. He shook his head, hardly able to believe what was happening.

'It's Tommy,' he managed to gasp out. 'My brother Tommy. He's not dead after all. We got a telegram this morning, from the War Office. He's a prisoner of war in Germany.'

Finally recognising Peter and Hannah on the far side of the classroom he broke off.

128

'Did you hear?' he called to them. 'Tommy's alive.'

Peter got to his feet and crossed over to Jack. He put his hand on his friend's arm and squeezed.

'That's marvellous news. Is he well?'

'We think so. They said he got wounded in the retreat to Dunkirk. He's been in a German hospital for the past few months. That's why we didn't hear before. But he's better now. He's in a prisoner of war camp with all the rest of his regiment.'

It took nearly ten minutes for Jack to calm down. Mrs Stephens was patient, knowing how important the news was for the boy. So she let him chatter on while the rest of the class concentrated on their reading books. And slowly but surely Jack grew calmer.

'Ready for work now?' asked Mrs Stephens.

Jack nodded. He bent his head over his book, breathing deeply through his mouth, happy for the first time in months.

'Bet they'll never hold him in that prison camp,' he whispered suddenly. 'He'll escape, you'll see!'

Peter started to chuckle. It was infectious and soon the whole room was rocking with laughter. Mrs Stephens knew when she was beaten. Smiling to herself, she lay down her book.

'All right,' she called. 'Ten minutes on the playground – all of you. And Jack? Make sure you're ready for work the moment you get back.'

As the class crowded for the door she lay back in her chair and sighed happily. This was just the news that all of them needed. It looked as if Christmas had come early after all.

Chapter Ten

On the day before New Year's Eve, Hannah woke early. It was still dark and a thin rain pattered against the windowpane. She turned over in bed, snuggling down amongst the blankets and eiderdown. From the rooms below she heard the wireless playing – her mother was obviously already up and about.

Reluctantly, Hannah pushed back the covers and climbed out of bed. She shivered as her feet touched the cold oilcloth and quickly reached for her slippers. Then, pulling on her dressing gown, she went downstairs.

'Hello, love,' called her mother. 'Sorry. Did I wake you? I'm just making breakfast. Do you want some toast?'

Hannah nodded and sat down at the table. On the wireless the news was just beginning.

'Last night,' came the voice of the announcer, 'heavy air raids are reported to have taken place on the city of London. In attacks that lasted many hours, thousands of incendiary and high explosive bombs were dropped from wave after wave of enemy planes. Over 1500 fires were started in the city and docks area.'

Mrs Roberts came in from the kitchen with a freshly brewed pot of tea. She paused to listen to the news.

'Sounds to me like the second Great Fire of London!' she said. 'They really are taking a pasting.'

Hannah frowned at her mother's words and tried to

keep down the feeling of unease in her chest and belly. Don't be silly, she told herself, bombing raids have been taking place for months now, this one won't be any different from the rest.

'What are you planning to do today?' asked Mrs Roberts, switching off the wireless and quickly changing the subject.

Hannah shrugged and helped herself to a piece of toast. Her mother passed across the rhubarb jam she and Hannah had made together in the summer.

'Jack and Peter are coming round later. We've got a project to finish for school. I said we could sit and do it in the front room. Is that all right?'

Mrs Roberts smiled at her daughter.

'Of course it is. Right, I'm off to work. Make sure the fire in the front room is lit before the boys get here. I'll see you tonight.'

She bent and kissed Hannah lightly on the top of her head.

'Don't worry about Helen. I'm sure she'll be fine.'

When Jack and Peter arrived a few hours later they were excited and noisy. Jack didn't know what to talk about first, the model tank he'd been given for Christmas, his brother Tommy in the prisoner-of-war camp or the air raid on London the night before.

'It's New Year's Eve tomorrow,' he cried, delightedly. 'Then it's 1941. Imagine that, the year 1941. We'll give them what for next year, you wait and see. This year we won the Battle of Britain. Soon we'll win the Blitz as well. I reckon it'll all be over by next Christmas.'

'I wouldn't be too sure,' said Peter. 'This war will probably last a long, long time – maybe even long enough for you to join up, eh Jack?'

He nudged his friend, playfully, in the ribs. Jack's eyes gleamed with expectation. He could hardly wait.

*   *   *

They went back to school a few days later. The weather was cold and wet and their first day was spent clustered around the ancient stove at the front of the classroom. The supply of coke was limited and it gave off very little warmth. All day they shivered and pulled their coats tightly around themselves. Lessons held little interest and Hannah longed for Spring. She wanted warmth for her frozen body.

Hannah came home from school to find her mother seated in the kitchen. She still wore her scarf and coat.

'What are you doing here?' Hannah asked. 'You aren't meant to be home for hours yet.'

Mrs Roberts smiled, faintly. It took effort and, immediately, Hannah sensed that something was wrong.

'What is it? What's the matter?'

Her mother stood up, took Hannah by the shoulders and guided her to a chair. Standing above her daughter, she clearly found it difficult to speak. And in that moment Hannah knew.

'It's Helen, isn't it?'

Mrs Roberts nodded, slowly and deliberately.

'I'm sorry, love. Her aunt came down to the factory to see me. She wanted you to know and thought I was the best one to tell you. They think . . . they think . . .'

She paused and turned away towards the window, unable to continue.

'Helen's dead?' whispered Hannah.

She reached out and grabbed her mother's arm, desperate to know the answer to her question. Mrs Roberts nodded.

'I think so. That's what her aunt said.'

A huge echoing emptiness had suddenly closed down upon Hannah's chest. It was what she had been dreading for months now. Poor Helen, she thought. Poor frightened, brave Helen.

And then came the guilt. I should have persuaded her to stay here with us, she told herself. I should have kept her here where she'd have been safe. It's my fault. My fault she's dead. A sudden panic began to claw at her throat, the bile rising and filling her nose and mouth. It was choking her.

With a cry, Hannah leapt to her feet and ran to the kitchen sink. There she was sick, suddenly and violently sick. For two minutes the spasm lasted, before she was finally able to stand up and stagger back to her seat.

'How did it happen?' she gulped. 'When?'

'Just before New Year. Remember the incendiary raids? Helen was at home. They had no Anderson Shelter. A bomb landed on the house. A direct hit.'

Hannah sat with her eyes lowered, her mind full of memories – Helen on the hill above Langland Bay, Helen sitting and laughing in Conti's Café, Helen frightened but still walking with her as they followed 'the spy who wasn't'.

'She wouldn't have known anything about it, love,' said Mrs Roberts. 'A direct hit. The whole house came down. It would have been very quick.'

The pain in Hannah's belly and chest was real and livid. And yet there was something else, something strange and indefinable, something she couldn't quite place. She shook her head, desperately trying to clear her mind.

'Let yourself cry, Hannah,' said Mrs Roberts. 'You'll feel better if you let it all go.'

Again Hannah shook her head.

'No, mum. There's something –.'

She pushed herself onto her feet and crossed to the window.

'Have they buried her yet? I mean, is it all over?'

Mrs Roberts was flustered now. This wasn't the way she had expected things to go, not by a long shot.

'No – no, love. They haven't found her body yet.'

Hannah suddenly cried out aloud, then clamped her hand across her mouth. This was it, this was what had been troubling her. Now she knew.

'There would have been so much rubble and debris, Hannah,' said her mother. 'It could take weeks to clear all that and to – well – find her.'

Hannah stared at her mother and then, slowly, began to smile.

'No, mum. It's going to be all right. You said it yourself. They haven't found her. They haven't found her body. She'll be alive, believe me.'

Mrs Roberts frowned, then moved forward to seize her daughter by the shoulders. She pulled Hannah round and stared into her eyes.

'Hannah, be sensible. I know this is a shock, love, but it's been almost a week . . .'

'Let me finish, Mum. I know Helen's alive, I really do. She's strong, in a way that other people can't see, in a way others don't know. She's got to be alive. She's got to come back and see me.'

She pulled herself away from her mother's clasping hands and moved quickly towards the front door.

'Where are you going, Hannah?'

Hannah felt the power and the belief running through her body. She turned.

'I'm going to tell Peter and Jack. They need to know. And it's better if it comes from me.'

'Do you want me to come with you?'

Hannah shook her head.

'No. I think I'd like to be on my own for a bit.' She smiled back at her mother. 'It'll be all right, Mum. I promise.'

She went out, leaving Mrs Roberts staring at her daughter's departing back in disbelief.

*   *   *

Hannah walked to school early the following morning. Peter and Jack had been stunned when she had broken the news – unlike Hannah, they could not believe that Helen had, somehow, managed to survive the air raid.

135

'It's been nearly a week now,' Peter had protested, logical as ever. 'Even if she was alive after the bomb blast, she'd have been without food and water for days.'

Hannah had simply smiled at him.

'I know. Don't ask me to explain it but I know she's alive. Just because we haven't heard, it doesn't mean she hasn't been found. I know she's alive, Peter, I just know it.'

That night, however, in the long hours of darkness, even she began to doubt. It was such a long time and if Helen hadn't been killed by the bomb she might even have suffocated to death. All night Hannah tossed and turned, her mind fluctuating between disbelief and wild hopes. Only with the coming of morning did her courage return.

She found Mrs Stephens in the staff room and quickly told her the news. The teacher was shocked and concerned.

'I think you should go home, Hannah. We all know what Helen meant to you.'

Hannah shook her head.

'No, thank you, Miss. Helen was brave, probably the bravest person I've ever known. Now I'm going to be brave for her. It'll be all right, Miss. She isn't dead.'

Mrs Stephens stared at her.

'But Hannah, it's been almost a week.'

The teacher's eyes were brimming with tears.

'I don't care!'

Hannah's voice had begun to rise. She felt something fluttering in her throat, some vague emotion rising, threatening to overwhelm her – a tide of water that she knew she had to keep down. She turned and went out to the playground.

When the class filed into the room to begin lessons for the day, Mrs Stephens called everyone to attention. They saw her face and knew that she had something important to say.

'I have some sad news to tell you,' announced the teacher, gravely. 'Here in Mumbles we are lucky – the war has hardly touched us yet. But we all know how badly London has suffered. Helen Lewis was here with us for a while, as an evacuee. Last year, she decided to go back home.'

She paused and stared at Hannah. From around the classroom heads turned to follow her gaze.

'Last night,' Mrs Stephens continued, 'we heard some terrible news. Helen has been killed in an air raid.'

A gasp went up from the class as the news hit home. Hannah shook her head.

'No, Miss,' she whispered, 'not killed. She's not dead.'

Only those closest to her heard Hannah's words. One or two girls began to cry but nobody spoke. The shock was like a blanket dropped suddenly over their heads. For twenty seconds nobody moved. And then, suddenly, there was a different sound in the room – laughter.

Hannah swung around. Sitting at his desk against the partition wall, Godfrey Scrivens was grinning and chuckling to himself. He looked up and saw Hannah staring at him. Slowly, deliberately, he drew his index finger across his throat.

'Dirty 'vacee,' he mouthed. 'Serves her right!'

His words, whispered as they were, echoed around the room. Mrs Stephens and all of the class sat shocked and speechless. Then a chair rasped across the floor. The noise was like a machine gun in the quiet room. Hannah saw Jack rise to his feet. Slowly, carefully, he walked across the room to Godfrey's desk and punched him, hard, on the nose.

Blood spurted from Godfrey's face and he fell back in his chair.

'Oh,' he screamed. 'My nose, my nose!'

He crouched back behind his raised hand, protecting himself from further attack. Blood streamed out between his fingers and tears began to course down his cheeks. Jack stared at him, impassively.

'That's from Helen,' he hissed.

He turned and went slowly back to his seat. All over the room children stared at Jack. The small boy was breathing heavily between tight lips. Godfrey lay, cowering and crying, in his seat. Mrs Stephens came slowly down the aisle and pulled him roughly to his feet.

'I am taking Godfrey to the staff room, to see to his injuries. No talking while I am gone.'

She went to the door, paused and then glanced briefly back into the room.

'Wash your hand, Jack,' she said, quietly. 'It's got blood on it.'

*   *   *

Saturday dawned bright and cold and Hannah was woken early by her mother. It had been a difficult week. The sorrow and the pain were constantly there but she had steadfastly refused to cry. There seemed to be a steadily rising tide behind her eyes, but she refused to let it out. It was something she felt that she owed to her friend, almost as if by not breaking down in despair her strength would, somehow, keep Helen safe.

In her dreams that night she and Helen, Jack and Peter, had been sitting in Mr Conti's café, watching holiday makers pass the window towards Mumbles Pier. Amongst the crowd she had seen Godfrey Scrivens, Trotty Truman and even their old spy from the woods. And then her mother shook her by the shoulder and woke her.

'Hannah, Mrs Livingstone, Helen's aunt, is here to see you. Get dressed, dear.'

Mrs Livingstone was sitting in the kitchen, drinking a cup of tea. Despite the depth of gloom inside her Hannah could not help smiling. No matter how bad the food shortages might be, any visitor to the house would always be sure of a cup of tea and a piece of cake from Mrs Roberts.

'Hello, Hannah,' said Helen's aunt.

She held out her hand, formally. Hannah shook it and sat down on the chair opposite.

'Mrs Livingstone has something to tell you, dear,' said her mother.

Hannah glanced at Helen's aunt, then at her mother. The huge well of water lurched and then steadied behind her eyes. She stared at Mrs Livingstone's face and began to smile.

'I know, Mum, I know what it is. Helen's alive, isn't she?'

Mrs Livingstone nodded.

'Yes, Hannah. They found her, under the rubble, two days ago.'

The wall of water was huge now, like a reservoir threatening to burst out over the dam. Mrs Livingstone leaned forward and took hold of Hannah's hands.

'She was under the table, in the Morrison Shelter. The house came down on top of her – and on the shelter, too. But it kept her safe. I suppose the table acted as a kind of barrier, like a beam. Just like it was meant to. There was a burst water main running right past the spot where she was lying. It kept Helen alive until, at last, somebody found her.'

'But how long was she there?' asked Hannah's mother.

'Three, maybe four, days. They say it's a miracle. They'd almost given up hope – well, there's so much to do, trying to repair the damage and rescue all those people. There was a small boy, playing in the rubble. He heard Helen shouting and the ARP men managed to dig her out.'

'And the rest of the family?'

Mrs Livingstone sadly shook her head. She reached into her pocket and pulled out an envelope.

'Helen's in hospital. And she will be for some time. But she sent this for you, Hannah. She wanted me to give it to you.'

140

She passed across the small brown packet. Hannah's stomach lurched as she recognised Helen's writing and the wall of water slid towards the top of the dam. Hand trembling, she turned the envelope over in her hand and stared, hardly comprehending, at the two women in front of her.

'Why don't you read the letter, dear?'

Hannah's head jerked upwards. She blinked hard to keep back the tears.

'I will, Mum. But not here. I've got to go out. I'll take it with me to read. I won't be long.'

Her mother nodded and understood. Hannah went out of the back door and pulled her bike from the garden shed. There was only one place to read the letter. Five minutes hard pedalling over the headland brought her to Langland Bay and there, sitting on the bank where she had first seen Helen all those months ago, she carefully slit open the envelope.

'Dear Hannah,' she read. 'This is just a quick letter. I've dictated it to one of the nurses as my arm was broken in the bombing and I still can't write yet.

'I just wanted you to know that I'm all right. No, it's more than that. During the time I was buried in the rubble I really thought I was going to die. I could have given up many times. That would have been so easy. But then I'd think of you. You and Peter and Jack – but mostly you. I remembered your strength, your determination, Hannah. And I knew that you wouldn't want me to give up. I don't know why but, for some reason, I felt you were thinking about me, too.

'So I kept going because I knew you'd want me to. And it worked, didn't it? When I get out of here they're going to send me to the country to get well. Then I'm coming back, to live with my aunt again. And this time I'm going to stay. Write to me, Hannah, please? I need to hear from you and the boys.

'And think about me because I never stop thinking about you.

All my love

Helen.

PS Tell Jack I've got some really great bits of shrapnel for his collection.'

Hannah let the letter drop onto her lap and, at last, the wall of water burst from behind her eyes. She cried, huge sobs of emotion wracking her body. She cried for her friend's loss. She cried because, late one summer, her country had gone to war. She cried because her childhood was over.

She read Helen's letter once more. 'Dear Hannah . . . I just wanted you to know that I'm all right.'

And then, to her own surprise, she was smiling and shaking her head in amazement. She began to laugh, slowly at first, but soon she was rocking back and forth, alternating between tears and hysteria. Helen was safe and coming back. Hannah would help her – and Peter and Jack, they would all help her – to come to terms with her loss. Whatever it took, they would help her.

Hannah reached for her bike and pushed it back along the path to the road. It was high time she saw the boys: at last she had some good news for them.

Other books by Phil Carradice

Novels
The Bosun's Secret
The Pirates of Thorne Island

Poetry
Ghostly Riders

Stories
'The Village that Lost its Dragon'
in *Dragon Days* ed. Brett Breckon

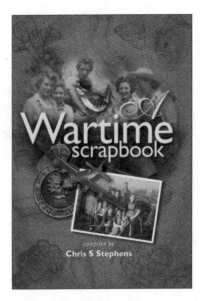

'Being a war baby was just hard luck' – or was it? Children growing up in wartime were certainly kept busy. They could be building a shelter, Digging for Victory in an allotment, taking a day off school for potato-picking, even befriending an evacuee. They had tasks to do – because many fathers were away at war and mothers working in weapons factories or perhaps driving lorries.

A Wartime Scrapbook will give children of the twenty-first century a vivid picture of the Second World War. It is a book for whole families to explore together, especially if grandparents or elderly relatives have memories of their own to share.

Chris Stephens, author of the popular anthologies *A Christmas Box* and *A Seaside Treat*, once again brings social history to life for readers of all ages.

Softback ISBN 1 84323 285 5	£5.99
Hardback ISBN 1 84323 390 8	£8.99